American Histories

John Edgar Wideman's books include *Writing to Save a Life, Philadelphia Fire, Brothers and Keepers, Fatheralong, Hoop Roots* and *Sent for You Yesterday*. He is a MacArthur Fellow and has won the PEN/Faulkner Award twice and has been a finalist for the National Book Critics Circle Award and National Book Award. In 2017, Wideman won the Prix Femina Étranger for *Writing to Save a Life*. He divides his time between New York and France.

'Wideman's rage against American injustice and racial prejudice burns magma-hot in his latest short stories . . . Challenging, animating, enlivening and electrifying; it does what literature should do. It's a bruising experience that leaves you feeling vulnerable and excited and alive'
Spectator

'Profound . . . Wideman's courage, his gorgeous plain speaking, is triumphant; it is a courage which almost allows the reader to believe that language can conquer despair, though despair is always evident . . . As Wideman has shown in book after book, it is the imagination that can allow a space in which a new understanding of all our stories may be forged – and where a more just future may be created'
New Statesman

'Wideman is one of the nation's literary treasures, and his contribution is a dazzling, delirious achievement: as his narrator, perched on the edge of the Williamsburg Bridge, prepares for suicide, he delivers a *cri de coeur* that ranges from Sonny Rollins to the Yalu River and becomes nothing less than a meditation on the extraordinary resilience of ordinary black lives in the American Century'
Junot Díaz

'Race and its reverberations are at the core of this slim, powerful volume, a blend of fiction, memoir, and reimagined history, in which the boundaries between those forms are murky and ever shifting . . . Lucid and strong . . . Arresting'
Boston Globe

ALSO BY JOHN EDGAR WIDEMAN

Fanon: A Novel

Briefs: Stories

God's Gym: Stories

The Island: Martinique

Hoop Roots: Basketball, Race, and Love

Two Cities: A Novel

The Cattle Killing: A Novel

Fatheralong: A Meditation on Fathers and Sons, Race and Society

All Stories Are True

The Stories of John Edgar Wideman

Philadelphia Fire: A Novel

Fever: Stories

Reuben: A Novel

Brothers and Keepers: A Memoir

Sent for You Yesterday: A Novel

Damballah: Stories

Hiding Place: A Novel

The Lynchers: A Novel

Hurry Home: A Novel

A Glance Away: A Novel

Writing to Save a Life: The Louis Till File

American Histories

JOHN EDGAR
WIDEMAN

CANONGATE

This paperback edition published in 2019 by Canongate Books

First published in Great Britain in 2018 by Canongate Books Ltd,
14 High Street, Edinburgh EH1 1TE

canongate.co.uk

1

Versions of "Williamsburg Bridge" and "JB & FD"
previously appeared in *Harper's Magazine*

First published in 2018 in the United States by Scribner,
an imprint of Simon & Schuster

British Library Cataloguing-in-Publication Data
A catalogue record for this book is available on
request from the British Library

ISBN 978 1 78689 208 9

Printed and bound in Great Britain by Clays Ltd, Elcograf S.p.A.

To C—

Luv, J

I do not know why this double-entry account of time intrigues me, and why I am compelled to call attention to it—to both its personal and objective forms, the time in which the narrator moves and that in which his narrative takes place. It is a peculiar intertwining of time's courses, which are ordained moreover to be bound up with yet a third—that is, with the time the reader will one day take for a receptive reading of what is told here, so that he will be dealing with a threefold ordering of time: his own, that of the chronicler, and that of history.

—Thomas Mann, *Doctor Faustus*

CONTENTS

American Histories

A PREFATORY NOTE

Dear Mr. President,

I send this note along with some stories I've written, and hope you will find time in your demanding schedule to read both note and stories. The stories should speak for themselves. The note is a plea, Mr. President. Please eradicate slavery.

I am quite aware, sir, that history says the Thirteenth Amendment to the Constitution abolished slavery in the United States of America in 1865, and that ensuing amendments extended to former slaves the precious rights and protections our nation guarantees to all its citizens regardless of color. But you should understand better than most of us, Mr. President, that history tells as many lies as truths.

The Thirteenth Amendment announced the beginning of the end of slavery as a legal condition in America. Slavery as a social condition did not disappear. After serving our nation for centuries as grounds to rationalize enslavement, African ancestry and colored skin remain acceptable reasons for the majority of noncolored Americans to support state-sponsored, state-enforced segregation, violence, and exploitation. Skin color continues to separate some of us into a category as unforgiving as the label property *stamped on a person. Dividing human beings into immutable groups identifiable by skin color reincarnates scientifically discredited myths of race. Keeps alive the unfortunate presumption, held by many of my fellow citizens, that they belong to a race granted a divine right to act as judges, jurors, and executioners of those who are members of other incorrigibly different and inferior races.*

What should be done, Mr. President. Our nation is deeply unsafe. I feel threatened and vulnerable. What can I do. Or you. Do we need another Harpers Ferry. Do we possess in our bottomless arsenal a weapon to demolish lies that connect race, color, and slavery.

By the time this note reaches your desk, Mr. President, if it ever does, you may be a woman. No surprise. Once we had elected a colored President, the block was busted. Perhaps you are a colored woman, and that would be an edifying surprise.

This note is getting too long. And to be perfectly honest, Mr. President, I believe terminating slavery may be beyond even your vast powers. My guess is that slavery won't disappear until only two human beings left alive, neither one strong enough to enslave the other.

Anyway, please read on and enjoy the stories that follow. No strings attached. No obligation to free a single slave of any color, Ms. or Mr. President.

JB & FD

1

To need his glasses and be struck by an awareness that they are not at hand, an ordinary-enough circumstance for Frederick Douglass, except sometimes it's accompanied by a flash of extraordinary dread. If not quite panic, certainly an unease disproportionate to a simple recurring situation. Dread that may be immediately extinguished if he locates his horn-rimmed, owlish-eyed spectacles exactly where he anticipated they should be.

He sees them and almost sighs. Nearly feels their slightly uncomfortable weight palpable on his nose. Finding the glasses is enough to reassure him that he remains here among the living in this material world where he depends on glasses to read, glasses to help him negotiate stubbornly solid objects he cannot glide through. Enough to remember that he's able to recall or backtrack, anyway, and understand how the present moment connects to moments preceding it, a trail of hows and whys causing him to wind up where he is now, at this particular moment, stretching out a hand to pick up eyeglasses because he is the same person who placed them on the desk, beside a stack of three books at the desk's upper-left-hand corner so he wouldn't forget, and there, here they would be when he needed glasses.

Sometimes dread does not vanish when he locates his glasses. They turn up where he thinks they should, his fingers curl, prepare to reach out for them. But glasses are not enough. Not convincing enough. They do not belong to him. Not glasses. Not hand. He vaguely recognizes both. Glasses too heavy to lift. Or hand too heavy. He's observing from an incalculable distance. Sometimes that detachment is a gift, sometimes it dooms him, and he cannot animate or orchestrate what he desires to come next. John Brown spreads his ancient, musty wool cloak—cloak the brown color of his name—over glasses, books, desk, study, house, wife, him, and when John Brown snatches the cloak away, nothing's there. Douglass has fled to the mountains, the woods to join him.

2

Ah, Frederick, my friend. Look at you, Fred Douglass. I knew after a single glance you could be the one. Your manly form and bearing left no room for doubt. And today, these dozen hard years later, you still stand tall, straight, gleaming. I see God's promise of freedom in you. Yours. Mine. Our nation's. A man who could lead his people, all people, out of slavery's bondage. Your beard dark that day we first spoke and now tinged with spools of gray, but you gleam still, my friend. Despite the iron cloud of suffering and oppression slavery casts over this land.

Douglass remembers no beard. Not wearing one himself, nor a beard on Brown's gaunt face. Certainly not the patriarch's thicket of white flowing—no, a torrent—today, halfway down John Brown's chest. He misremembers me.

But if God ignites a man to believe himself a prophet, if visions burst upon him and seize him, as an ordinary man is seized by a roiling gut and must rush behind a bush to squat and relieve himself, if such urgency is the case, I suppose, Douglass instructs himself, a prophet can be forgiven for mistaking petty details. Prophecies forgiven for confusing time and place, for compounding truth and error, wisdom and foolishness, for mixing wishful thinking with logic. John Brown thus forgiven for believing that ignorant, isolated slaves, cowed into submission by a master's whip, will grasp the purpose of a raid on Harpers Ferry and flock instantly to his banner. Enraptured by his vision, Brown foresees colored slaves armed with sticks and stones prevailing against cannons, Sharps carbines, the disciplined troops of a nation dedicated absolutely to upholding the principle that color makes some men less equal than others. I embrace the fiery justness of John Brown's prophecies, his unflinching willingness to sacrifice himself and his sons, yet I cannot forgive my friend for untempered speech, demagoguery, the impetuosity and rage that grip him. That transform dream to madness.

3

Douglass watches himself step out from behind the curtain and stride to the bunting-draped podium. They will welcome him. He is famous. Broad chest bemedaled, gold baton, field marshal's crimson sash decorating his resplendent uniform, veteran of a terrible war, though he never fired a shot in anger. Fine figure of a man still. After seven decades on earth. After a protracted, blood-drenched conflict settling nothing. Certainly not settling his fate. Nor his color's fate. Nor his nation's.

A drumroll of applause greets him, deepening as he moves step-by-step across the stage, a thunder of hands accompanying him. In the front rows his new white wife's white women friends. When a journalist asked Douglass to speak about his marriage, seeking details to spice the story he intended to write about newlyweds whose union scandalously ignored great disparities of age and race, Douglass replied, "My first wife the color of my mother, second the color of my father."

Tonight in this hall where he'd spoken once before, where once he'd been property, a fugitive hosted by abolitionists, a piece of animated chattel curiously endowed with speech, tonight in this hall he would address "The Woman Question." Proclaim every woman's God-granted entitlement, like his, to all the Rights of Man.

A born orator. Born with that gift and many glorious others, his mother assured him in stories told at night, whispering while she lay next to him in the darkness, their only time together, half hours she stole from her master, slipping away to walk an hour each way, plantation to plantation, to earn their half hour.

Second rumble of applause when he concludes his remarks. Head bowed, he waves away the noise and stirs it, conducts it, loves it even as his gesturing arm seems dismissive, seems modest, a humble man, a veteran tempering, allaying the crowd's enthusiasm just as he strokes and soothes and quiets and fine-tunes his new young wife's pale hair and pale skin, her passion that makes him tender, wistful, as often as aroused. These happy newlyweds. Her ferocious coven of female friends among the loudest of clappers.

The evening will be a success, and he will return home to drop dead. Douglass dead as suddenly as Lincoln felled by an assassin's bullet. Except the president lingered. Douglass won't. Dead. He sees this as surely as he sees his old face in the vanity mirror in their freshly papered bedroom. As surely as old man Brown saw blood. Only pools, rivers, an ocean of blood, John Brown swore, would cleanse the sin of man-stealing. No. Not cleanse. Not expunge or redeem or expiate. No. Blood must be shed. No promises. No better, cleaner South or North. Only a simple certainty that blood must be shed. Douglass read that dire text in Brown's distracted gaze, his stare. Same fire in himself as a boy who struck back, no fear of consequences, at bullying slave driver Covey. Same fire fanned by waves of hands striking hands that primes him, guides, draws him as he crosses to a podium. Fire in the young woman he's taken after forty years with his colored first wife, this second wife who will discover him lying comfortably on the floor as he would have been lying comfortably across their canopied bed awaiting her had his heart not stopped and dropped him like an ax drops an ox, Douglass lying there on the Turkish carpet he sees so clearly now and never will again. Won't see it when he falls, when the abyss blackens suddenly and his head slams down into the rug's elaborately woven prayers.

4

Through a smallish window in a small motel I watched snow falling, a heavy snow, probably more than enough coming down to transform in a couple of hours the unprepossessing landscape framed within the motel window. Big white flakes dropping effortlessly from the sky as I'd hoped all morning words would materialize on the page while I sat here in this unprepossessing room attempting to imagine a boy alone on a wilderness trail who drives his father's cattle along a shore of Lake Erie. How many miles there and back to supply a military encampment during the War of 1812, the boy on a horse or a mule, I assume, although it's possible he may have been on foot, armed with a long stick or a cudgel to protect himself and prod the stream of cattle along whichever edge of Lake Erie he advances—north, south, east, west—from Hudson, a small, new town in Ohio's Western Reserve, where the boy's family resides, to a base on the Detroit front occupied by a General Hull and his troops.

I had never been a white teenager with a strict, pious Calvinist father named Owen Brown whom I had accompanied often on cattle drives, never punched cows alone, never a slave like the boy his age John Brown immediately would befriend and never forget, the colored boy encountered in an isolated cabin located somewhere along his route. Very likely John Brown himself couldn't say exactly where, disoriented by an unexpected snowstorm that erased the usual familiar terrain and forced him for caution's sake to seek shelter for his animals and himself before nightfall, before he found himself lost completely, not sure how far he may have drifted from the trail, not even clear in which direction the trail might lie after hours of thick, swirling snow, certain of nothing but snow, wind, chilling cold, and the necessity to keep track of the cattle, perhaps round them up, count them, maybe drive them into a tight circle for warmth, cows huddled, hunkered down in a ring, and maybe him or him and his horse or mule bedded down close enough to share the heat of three, five, seven large beasts in a heap, a dark snowdrift in the middle of nowhere. Or perhaps drawn by the sight of a cabin ahead, you keep the animals moving as best you can and ride towards it, then dismount, or you've been plodding on foot and you reach a door and knock, embolden yourself, a shy, stranded twelve- or thirteen-year-old, to share the unhappy story of your plight, the errand your father entrusted to you, his livestock, his livelihood, delivering beef for General Hull's soldiers to eat so the Brown family can eat, so there's food on the table back in Hudson. Not army beef—cornmeal mush his mother measures, spoons out to John Brown and his siblings Ruth, Salmon, Oliver, and Levi Blakeslee, an orphan who, thanks to Owen Brown's charitable heart, was adopted and traveled as part of the Brown family to Hudson from New York State. Taut, hungry, lean faces at home, and now John Brown's duty to feed them.

Night deepening. Storm trapping him, a boy who's desperately seeking assistance, refuge, only or at least till daylight and he can relocate trail or landmarks and be on his way. I compare his predicament to mine, and I'm ashamed. My problem simply finding words, simply pretending to be in another time and place, another consciousness while settled in the comforts of a motel room along the interstate, fumbling around in storms of my own making, staring out a window at an increasingly postcard-perfect snowscape.

John Brown's storm does not subside but intensifies, lasting through the next afternoon perhaps, so he stays a night and half the following day in a cabin with a settler and his family, stranded here in a stranger's cabin for far too long, too far away from accomplishing his task. Owen Brown's cows outside maybe wandering off, lost in blinding snow. How many of them? Count them, band them together, search for strays, coax up the slovenly ones who otherwise would be content to die where they kneel, sunken into the snow.

These people are pioneers of sorts, like his, hovering at the edge of raw wilderness. Dark inside the cabin. Fireplace logs shiver, smolder, smoke. Spit loud as mountain streams thawing in spring. A question arising daily, as predictable as the sun: will they survive for another twenty-four hours on this not-quite-civilized frontier. Prayers each time they awaken, each time they break bread. Bread coarse, dark, hard, a little milk on occasion or water to soften it, a rare dab of honey to sweeten, or it's cornmeal porridge or cornmeal fried in grease to make a square of hot mush like John Brown receives that night in a cabin familiar to him from home, the wooden plates and heavy mush no strangers, nor the wife who smiles twice—John Brown notices, counts—during the hours of his stay.

She reminds him of his mother—busy without a pause, quiet as a shadow, a kindly shadow, she lets you know without saying a word, nor could you say how you know that deep kindness and deep fear hide inside her busyness. Her mouth like his mother's a tight line, lips nearly invisible even when she unseals them to address briskly, not often above a tight whisper, her three tiny girls or the man who is her husband, who's quite impressed by any youngish boy a father would trust to drive cattle along miles and miles of wilderness trail, a man who offers encouragement to John Brown to linger longer, though the boy and perhaps the host know he must refuse and he will, politely, this well-spoken boy. A boy who understands his mission. Determined, as long as he can draw breath into his body, to reach his destination and discharge his responsibilities. Then walk, ride, or crawl back to Hudson, money collected in hand. Hurry, hurry, not a moment to spare, so many crucial hours consumed, lost, wasted already.

Not a problem for me to identify with his anxious state of mind, his despondency and disappointment with himself, with John Brown's sense he could, should have been better prepared for any emergency that might sap precious time. His sister Ruth would not understand why her bowl is empty. Her big eyes, severe even when a very young child, hold back tears she knows better than to shed, not because she fears being disciplined for weeping at the dinner table—her parents love her, teach her, pray over her and with her every day. Tears would vex her mother, worry her father, tears might cause them to think she is blaming them for no food or, worse, blaming the Good Lord she knows is always watching over her, His grace abounding, more precious than thousands of earthly platters heaped with food.

John Brown imagines Ruth inside him and peeks out at himself with her deep, famished eyes, the way the slave boy looks at him, speaking with eyes, gestures, a silent conversation, a wordless friendship struck up with the first glances they exchange in the cabin, fellow outsiders, alien presences, raw boys of similar size, age.

* * *

John Brown winces but holds his tongue, his tears, when the dark boy cowers under a sudden flurry of blows, many thuds, cracks across his back, shoulders, arms, not ducking or fleeing, hands not thrust up to protect himself from blows delivered by a stout stick that must have been leaning against the head of the rough log table, stationed there at the man's hand, John Brown immediately perceives, for exactly this purpose. Rapid, loud blows that are—is it fair to suggest?—as painful in John Brown's mind as they are on the slave boy's body, fair to say the sting of this not-uncommon beating cools soon and is forgotten by a black boy's tough flesh, but a white boy's shock endures. Surprise, surprise for John Brown the evil in the heart of this grown-up man nothing but kind to him, offering succor from a storm to one of his kind, a stranger, a mere feckless boy who let down his father, his family. I've lost my way, good sir. A father like his father but unlike, too, as John Brown feels himself like and unlike the black slave boy his age who serves them, who eats and sleeps under the same roof with this family, with him that night, but in a corner. Eats over there, sleeping there under rags, rags his bedding, clothes, roof, walls, floor all nothing but rags, a dark mound of rags the wind has blown into the house perhaps when the door opened to let John Brown enter or leave or when the man who's father of the house passes in and out to piss or the slave boy's endless chores drive him into the storm to do whatever he's ordered to do until he's swept by a final gust of wind one last time back into the cabin, a piece of night, ash, cinder trying to stay warm in a corner where it lands.

5

Spring rains swelled the rivers the year my sons John and Jason set off to join their brothers in Kansas and be counted among antislavery settlers when the territory voted to decide its future as a free or slave state. They left Ohio with their families, traveling by boat on the Ohio, then Mississippi River to St. Louis, Missouri, where they bought passage on a steamer, the *New Lucy*, to reach the camp at Osawatomie that the family had taken to calling Brown's Station.

A long, cold, wet journey to Kansas, Douglass, and on the final leg God saw fit to take back the soul of my grandson, four-year-old Austin, Jason's elder son, stricken during an outbreak of cholera on board the steamer. When the boat docked at Waverly, Missouri, the grieving families of Jason and John, despite a drenching thunderstorm, disembarked to bury young Austin. The boat's captain, a proslavery man surrounded by his Southern cronies, the same ruffians who had brandished pistols and bowie knives, swearing oaths, shouting obscenities, swaggering, and announcing their bloody intent to make Kansas a slave state, the same brigands who had terrorized their fellow passengers night and day, singling out my sons, whose accent and manner betrayed them as Northerners. All those devils must have laughed with the captain at the cruel joke he bragged he was playing on the bereaved families, dumping their meager baggage to soak and rot on the dock, steaming away from Waverly before the distraught mourners returned from their errand, abandoning them during a downpour in a slave state though they had paid fares to Kansas.

* * *

No simple business to slaughter men with broadswords. To hack and slice human flesh with less ceremony than we butcher sheep and pigs. Dark that late night, early morning in Kansas when we descended upon homesteads of the worst proslavery vigilantes and fell to killing along Pottawatomie Creek. I was in command. Ordered the guilty to come out from their homes. Ordered executions in the woods. I knew the men I condemned had assaulted and murdered peaceful settlers, and among their victims were members of my family. Still, I stood aside at first, appalled by the fury, blood, screams, the mayhem perpetrated by weapons wielded by my sons Owen and Salmon and our companions. Though I entertained not the slightest of doubts, Frederick—the awful acts committed that day were justified, even if they moved the clock only one minute closer to the day our nation must free itself from the sin of slavery—yet I stayed my hand until the quiet of dawn had returned. Then, in silence broken only by pitiful moans, I delivered a pistol shot to the brain of a dying James Doyle.

6

Here is a letter (some historians call it fiction) written by Mahala Doyle in the winter of 1859 and delivered to John Brown awaiting execution in his prison cell in Virginia:

> *I do feel gratified to hear that you were stopped in your fiendish career at Harpers Ferry, with the loss of your two sons, you can now appreciate my distress in Kansas, when you . . . entered my house at midnight and arrested my Husband and two boys,*

and took them out of the yard and shot them in cold blood, shot them dead in my hearing, you can't say you done it to free slaves, we had none and never expected to own one, but has only made me a poor disconsolate widow with helpless children. . . . Oh how it pained my heart to hear the dying groans of my Husband & children.

7

On the road between Cleveland and Kansas, gazing up at the stars, John Brown's son Frederick said, "If God, then this. If no God, then this."

John Brown remembers the wonder in Frederick's voice, how softly, reverently his son spoke, so many stars overhead in the black sky, remembers the wagon wheels' jolt, yield, bounce had spun a seemingly unending length of rough fabric from the road's coarse thread, then a seamless, silky ride for John Brown lasting until Frederick's words returned him to an invisible chaos of slippery mud, rocks, craters that snatch them, tumble them, rattle their bones. Any moment a sudden, unavoidable accident might pitch both men overboard or smash the wagon to splinters as it traverses this broken section of road between Cleveland and Kansas, and there is no other road except the one spun for a few minutes during John Brown's forgiving sleep, his forgetful sleep.

How many minutes, hours, how much unbroken silence of sleep before he awakened abruptly to hear his son Frederick's voice asking how many miles covered, how many more miles to go to Kansas, Father. His poor, half-mad, feeble-brained son, the one of all his children, people agree, who resembles him most in face and figure, Fred, loyal and uncomplaining as a shoe. Tall, sturdy Frederick, who will die in a few weeks in Kansas. Dead once before as an infant, then reborn, rebaptized Frederick in remembrance of his lost little brother. Frederick's second chance to live cut short by ruffians in a border war, my second perished Frederick. Then a third chance, a dark son or dark father or mysteriously both, bearing the same Christian name my sons bore, Frederick, and John Brown trembles after his sleeping eyes pop open when he hears his son's declaration, Frederick's soft blasphemy revealing his wonder at a thought he had brewed all by himself while he drove the wagon transporting father and son to the killing fields of Missouri and Kansas, driving through this great holy world, this conundrum, John Brown thinks, far too perplexing, too fearful for a father to grasp or explicate.

In his cell in Virginia, John Brown will remember riding in a wagon at night with his dead son Frederick on the way to rejoin family in the camp in Kansas. His arm stiffens, his fist grips the hilt of an imaginary broadsword, and he mimics blows he witnessed in predawn darkness, blows his sons Salmon and Owen inflicted on outlaws they attacked on Pottawatomie Creek. This stroke for a dead grandson, Austin. This one for dead baby Frederick. This for Frederick who shared his lost brother's name and died too soon, twenty-six years old, in those Kansas Territory wars. And more blows struck for other, darker Fredericks, all of them his children, God's children, Brown almost shouts aloud as he presses again a revolver's actual barrel against the skull of whimpering, murdering night rider Doyle. An act of mercy or vengeance, he will ask God in his cell, to end the suffering of a nearly dead evil wretch when he pulls the trigger.

8

(1856)

Mrs. Thomas Russell wrote: *Our house was chosen as a refuge because no one would have dreamed of looking for Brown therein . . .*

John Brown stayed a week with us, keeping to his room almost always, except at meal time, and never coming down unless one of us went up to fetch him. He proved a most amiable guest, and when he left, I missed him greatly . . .

First time that I went up to call John Brown, I thought he would never open his door. Nothing ensued but an interminable sound of the dragging of furniture.

"I have been finding the best way to barricade," he remarked, when he appeared at last. "I shall never be taken alive, you know. And I should hate to spoil your carpet."

"You may burn down the house, if you want to," I exclaimed.

"No, my dear, I shall not do that."

Mrs. Russell goes on to record: *John Brown had the keenest possible sense of humor, and never missed the point of a joke or of a situation. Negroes' long words, exaggerations, and grandiloquence afforded him endless amusement, as did pretentiousness of any sort . . .*

He was acute in observing the quality of spoken English, and would often show himself highly diverted by the blunders of uneducated tongues. He himself spoke somewhat rustically, but his phrases were well formed, his words well chosen, and his constructions always forcible and direct. When he laughed he made not the slightest sound, not even a whisper or an intake of breath; but he shook all over and laughed violently. It was the most curious thing imaginable to see him, in utter silence, rock and quake with mirth. . . .

(1858)

John Brown thinks of it as molting. His feathers shed. A change of color. Him shriven. Cleansed. Pale feathers giving way to darker. Darker giving way to pale. Not seasonal, not a yearly exchange of plumage as God sees fit to arrange for birds or for trees whose leaves alter their hue before they drop each fall. His molting occurs in an instant. He stands naked. A tree suddenly stripped of leaves. Empty branches full again in the blink of an eye.

I see such alterations in myself, Douglass, in my dreams and often in God's plain daylight, and wonder if others notice my skin falling away, turning a different color, but I do not ask, not even my wife or children, for fear I will be thought mad. One more instance of insanity my enemies could add to discredit me. Old Brown thinks he changes colors like a bird or a leaf.

Free slaves, mad Brown shouts. Free the coloreds, as if color simply a removable outer shell, as if color doesn't permanently bind men into different kinds of men. As if feathers, leaves, fur, skin, fleece, all one substance, and all colors a single color. Yet I believe they are the same in God's eye.

I thank you again for the kindness and generosity you and your wife have extended towards me. I arrived here weary, despondent, exhausted by the Kansas wars, and you offered shelter. A respite from enemies who pursue me as if there's a price on my head here in the North as well as in the South. Your welcoming hand and spirit have revived me. I have been able to think. Write my Constitution.

When not occupied by my pen, I have benefited from your willing ear, your thoughtful responses to my poor attempt to draft a document that protects every American instead of a privileged few. I am eternally indebted to you for the sanctuary you provided, for your unceasing hospitality these last three weeks, and to demonstrate my gratitude, I'm ashamed to admit, I ask for even more from you. Not for myself this time, but for the grand cause we both are destined to serve. You must join us in Virginia, Frederick Douglass.

Why are you certain that my enslaved brethren will "hive" to you, as you put it. Why certain that a general insurrection will follow the Harpers raid and topple the South's slaveholding empire, free my people from bondage. I agree with much of your reasoning and share your sense of urgency, but do not share your certainty. Envy it, yes, but do not share it. You cite Toussaint's successful revolt in Haiti and Maroons free in the hills of Jamaica. Yet Virginia is not Jamaica, not Haiti. I believe there must be better ways than bloody rebellion to end the abomination of slavery. Why are you so certain God looks with favor on your plan. What if, despite your fervor and good intentions, you are wrong.

Wrong, you say. Wrong. In this nation where a man's color is reason enough to put him in chains. Where cutthroats in Kansas murder settlers whose only offense is hatred of slavery. Where a senator is caned in the halls of Congress for condemning man-stealers. In a nation where every citizen is compelled by law to aid and abet slave masters who seek to recover escaped "property," why is it difficult to separate right from wrong.

I tremble as I utter this chilling thought, Frederick Douglass, but what if no God exists except in the minds of believers. Would it not behoove us more, not less, to bear witness to what is right. To testify. To manifest, in our acts, the truth of our God's commandments.

I make no claim to be God's chosen warrior. I have studied an assault on the Virginia arsenal for a very long while. Devised a strategy I believe will exploit a powerful enemy's weaknesses. Recruited and trained good men to fight alongside me and my sons. Weighed both moral and practical consequences. Asked myself a thousand times what right do I have to commence such an undertaking. Still, I would be a fool to think I'm closer to knowing God's plan. We serve Him in the light or darkness of our understanding.

(1859)

Stand with us. You would be a beacon, Frederick. Let Southerners and Northerners, freemen and the enslaved, see the righteous power, the fierce, unquenchable spirit I recognized in you the first time we met. Let the world know that you are aroused, aggrieved. That you will not rest until your brethren are free. Teach your fellow countrymen there can be no peace, no forgiveness as long as slavery abides. Accompany us to Virginia. Strike a blow with us.

I must die one day, John Brown, sure enough. But I feel no need to hurry it. I don't reckon that ending my life in Virginia will make me a better man than one who chooses to survive and dedicates himself to serving God and his people. I shall continue my work here in the North. Offer my life, not my death, to my people.

I respect your well-known courage and principles. Nevertheless, I must speak bluntly, and say that I believe you quibble. You speak as if a man's time on earth is merely a matter of hours, days, years.

In this business we cannot afford to bargain. To quibble about more time, less time, a better time. We are not accountants, Fred. Duty requires more than crying out against slavery, more than attempting to maintain a decent life while the indecencies of slavery are rife about us. To rid the nation of a curse, blows must be struck. Blood shed. I am prepared to shed blood. Mine. My sons'.

And my blood. And the blood of young Green here, fresh from chains, who, after listening to us debate, not quibble, chooses to accompany you to Virginia.

Some days, I assure you, my feet, my mind rage. Yet a voice intercedes: do not give up hope for this intolerable world. Change must come. Like you, I believe the Good Lord in Heaven has grown impatient with this Sodom. Soon He may perform a cleansing with His glorious, stiff-bristled broom. I will rejoice if He calls me to that work.

I have made up my mind as you have made up yours, John Brown. And this man, Green, his mind. Godspeed to you both.

9

My name is John Brown and I want my son to hear the story of my name so I will talk the story to this good white lady promises she write down every word and send them in a letter to my son in Detroit on Pierce Road last I heard of him and his wife and three children, a boy, two girls, don't know much else about them, must be old by now, maybe those three children got kids and grandkids of they own and I never seen none them with my own two eyes, these old eyes bad now don't see much of anything no more, wouldn't hardly see them grands nor great-grands today if they standing here right beside this bed so guess I never will see them in this life and that fact makes me very sorry, son, and old-man sorry the worse kind of sorry, I believe, and let me tell you, my son, don't you dare put off to tomorrow because tomorrow not promised, tomorrow too late, too late, but don't need to tell you all that, do I, son, you ain't no spring chicken, you got to be old your ownself cause I comes into the world in eighteen and fifty-eight just before the war old John Brown started and seem like wasn't hardly no time before here you come behind me, me still a boy myself, but I want to tell you the story of my name not my age and how you supposed to know that story less I tell it and this nice lady write the words and maybe you read them one day to my grands and great-grands, son, then they know why John Brown my name and why John Brown a damn fine name, but listen, son, don't you ever put off to tomorrow trying to be a good man, a honest man, hardworking, loving man, don't put it off cause that gets a man in trouble, deep-down trouble, cause time is trouble, time full of trouble, and time on your hands when your hands ain't doing right fills up your time with trouble, then it's too late, your time to do right gone, you in the middle of doing evil or trying not to or trying to undo evil you done and time gone, too late, like me in a cage a dozen and some years locked up behind bars for killing a fella didn't even know his name till I hears it in the courtroom and lucky he black everybody say or you wouldn'a made it to no damn courtroom, no jail, crackers string your black ass up, the other prisoners say, you lucky nigger, they say, and cackle, grin, and shake they heads and moan and some nights make you want to cry like a baby all them long, long years when if I ain't slaving in the fields under a hellfire sun I'm sitting in a cell staring at a man's blood on a juke-joint floor, never get my time back once I yanks a bowie knife out my belt and he waving his knife and mine quicker finds his heart, the very same bowie knife my father Jim Daniels give to me and John Brown give to him, said, Use this hard, cold steel, Mr. Jim Daniels, on any man try to rob your freedom, same knife old John Brown stole from the crackers like he stole my daddy, mama, my sister and brother, and a passel of other Negroes from crackers down in Kansas and Missouri, it's too late, too late, knife in my hand, I watched a man bleed to death inside those stone walls every day year after year, hard time, son, you wait too long to do right it's too late and you can't do nothing, can't change time, and that's that, like the fact I never seen my grands, never seen you but once, one time up there on the Canada side in that cold and snow and wind, your mama carried you all them miles, had you wrapped up like you some little Eskimo or little papoose. It was only once only that one time I ever seen you, there you was with your mother, she come cross with you on the ferry, and me and her talked or mize well tell it like it was, she talked and I kinda halfway listened but I didn't want to hear nothing I wasn't ready to hear, nodded my head, smiled, chucked you under your chubby double chins, patted her shoulder, smooched her beautiful brown Indin-color colored cheek a couple times, always liked your mama, but the problem was I didn't know then what I know

now, son, or excuse me, yes I did, I knowed it just as clear as day, course I did, just didn't want to hear it cause I had other plans, knucklehead, young-blood plans, what I'ma do with a wife and baby, it was rough up there, barely feed myself, keep a roof over my head, if you could call a tent a roof, so how am I supposed to look out for youall, anyway, it was only that once I seen you, then same day she's back on the ferry, she's gone, you gone, nothing, no word for lots and lots of years cept a little tad or tidbit the way news come and go in prison or hear this or that happened from people passing through up there in Canada, me asking or somebody telling tales they don't even know my name who I am or know you or know who your mama and who you is to me or who my peoples is, but I'd overhear this or that in somebody's story and so in a manner of speaking I kept up, knew you still alive, then your mama dead and you married living on Pierce Road in Detroit, three grandkids I ain't never laid eyes on, never will now . . . Excuse me, Miss, you got that all down so far or maybe I should slow up or maybe just go ahead and shut up now, stop now cause how you think this letter find him anyway even if I say it right and you catch every word I say on paper it still don't sound right to me hearing myself talk this story, it just makes me sad, and it's a damned shame, a mess anyway, too late to tell my son my daddy, his granddaddy, Jim Daniels, give me John Brown's name because John Brown carried us out from slavery in the fall of 1858, my brother and sister, mama, and Jim Daniels, my father cross seven states, 1,100 miles, eighty-two days in wagons, railroad trains, on foot, boats, along with six other Negroes John Brown stole from slavery in Kansas and Missouri and Daddy say one them other six, a woman slave, ask John Brown, "How many miles, how many days, Captain Brown, we got to go before freedom?" and John Brown answer her and the lady slave say back, "That's a mighty far piece you say, Captain, sir. Ole Massa pitch him a terrible conniption fit we ain't back to fix his dinner," and then me born on one them last couple days before they cross the river to freedom, so my daddy Jim Daniels named me John Brown, he told me, and if I'da been more than half a man when you and your mama come up there I woulda took care of youall and passed my name on to you and you be another John Brown whatever else my sweet Ella called you you'd be John Brown, too, and if you knew the story of the name, son, maybe you would have passed the name on, too, John Brown, and maybe not, Miss, what do you think, Miss, is it too late, too much time gone by, Miss, what do you think.

10

Along an edge of the Gulf of Morbihan I walk through woods, on gravelly, rocky beaches, in sand, on a narrow walkway atop a mile-long stone seawall, then climb a bluff overlooking the wall where I can peer way, way out to dark clumps of island in the gulf's glittering water, towards open sea invisible beyond the islands. I imagine an actor assigned to deliver the colored John Brown monologue in a film version of "JB & FD." The actor asks me why I choose to make the nice lady in the script white, not colored. Asks why I invented a colored John Brown.

Powerful sea winds have shaped trees I stand next to on the bluff, winds that would shape me, too, no doubt, if I stood here very long. Trees with thick, ancient-looking gray trunks, bark deeply furrowed as old John Brown's skin, multiple trunks entwined, branches big as trunks, twisted, tortured, though a few trees shoot more or less straight up to vast crowns that form a layered green canopy of feathery needles high overhead. A row of maybe seven, eight survivors of probably hundreds of years of battering wind, and spaced among them another four or five cut down to stumps a couple yards across you could sit on and stare out at endless water beyond the edge of land, beyond the seawall and Roman ruins below.

Next to trees, still standing and fallen, I forget who I am, who I'm supposed to be, and it is perfection. Doesn't matter who I am or believed I was or all the shitty jobs performed to get to France—I listen for the voices of Frederick Douglass and John Brown sealed within the silence of those huge trees. Trees I don't know a name for, thinking maybe pine or fir or conifer, and I never will need to look up the name because for a small instant I'm inside them, and it lasts forever.

DARK MATTER

We go out to dinner and discuss eating.

We go out to dinner and discuss the economy's downswings and upswings.

We go out to dinner and discuss the importance of staying physically fit and the difficulties in busy, aging lives of maintaining a consistent, healthy program of exercise.

We go out to dinner and discuss Vladimir Putin's rumored kleptomania, how the U.S. State Department allegedly advises a famous coach who just returned from conducting basketball clinics in Russia that maybe the best course of action would be not to lodge a complaint with the UN about his NBA championship ring which had gone missing under extremely suspicious circumstances, while the coach was a guest at Putin's dacha, but to live and let live and they, the U.S. Government, would ante up for a replacement ring.

We go out to dinner and discuss choices after a waitress—long legs, minidress, coffee-au-lait-colored skin, intricately cornrowed hair—squatted in the darkness at the end of our table, peering over its edge as she articulated in her oddly precise diction subtleties we could anticipate, surprises far beyond anything words on the menu able to express. Wonderfully enticing items, she convinced us, not because we believed she'd peeked at the chef preparing them but because she was a tasty appetizer we were already sampling down there between our table and the next row of tables, her pretty legs folded under her, big eyes, pretty face popping up Kilroy-like where we had no reason to expect a face to be.

We go out to dinner and discuss public schools supposed to educate thirteen-year-old colored boys, public schools that taught them nothing, or schools anyway that did not teach them not to shoot each other inside school buses. Public schools where white cops learned it was okay to shoot down unarmed thirteen-year-old colored boys in the streets.

We go out to dinner and discuss growing up, the love-hate of family relationships, parents and parenting and learning to forgive mistakes, our parents' mistakes, our children's, our own, and why should anybody believe things might ever be different, people being people as far back in time as people remember, same ole, same ole selfishness, rivalries, cruelties unto death. A couple mornings after that night, I rode down in the elevator with my bagful of glass, plastic, cans, and miscellaneous other recyclables our building asks residents to sort out and deposit in slots in various colored containers in the basement, and on the way back up accidentally stopped one floor short of mine and risked knocking on 801's door, though it was Sunday and barely 10:00 A.M., but thank goodness, L responded almost immediately, almost as if she'd been awaiting my knock, and that sort of relieved the pressure, because it meant I was not necessarily disturbing a neighbor's sleep or privacy or worse. Without exchanging a single word with me, L went to fetch her husband, and suddenly there he was, beside her just outside the door, him puffy-faced, spiky hair askew, wearing a Peanuts pj top and sweatpants, me in cutoffs, T-shirt, standing in the hall, fresh from trash dumping, wondering why I'd knocked. Then L with a stoic smile moved a few steps backward into the apartment so we—two upper-middle-class, differently colored, orphaned males—could hug. As we separated, nothing to say. He knows I must know his father gone now like mine. Dead in Dublin from a stroke suffered the same night we had been out to dinner in a restaurant and he had discussed his father's loneliness since losing his wife of fifty years, his father's helplessness, speechlessness palpable while they spoke on the phone.

We go out to dinner and discuss relativity, dark matter, climate change, the origins and inevitable demise of the life-form we represented, our guilt collectively or individually, yea or nay, for circumstances in which we find ourselves.

We go out to dinner and discuss *Breaking Bad*, the nationwide epidemic of crystal meth, rural versus urban poverty, the former attorney general's height, the INS, IRS, ISIS, bedbug-sniffing dogs.

We go out to dinner and discuss those missing.

We go out to dinner and discuss us, the ones present who weren't so bad off, after all, if we looked at the options.

* * *

We go out to dinner and discuss retirement and my old buddy sitting across the table from me laughs loudly at himself laughing at me, grad students in Spain where some Spaniards called me El Moro, and one called me a big Chinaman, me laughing and splashing around once in a puddle of my vomit several feet deep according to my old buddy. His vomit, too, he boasted, him laughing and splashing in it, too, and why in the world, what in the world, what got into us, man, back in the day, what were we thinking, man, all that booze, booze, booze like no tomorrow.

We go out to dinner and discuss the Twin Towers, and they trundle through the restaurant door in blackface, huffing and puffing past a crowd of multicolored patrons to pull up chairs and sit at our table, cute lobster bibs tied round their necks, smoking cigars in a clearly marked no-smoking zone, two good ole boys just happy to be out and chilling in a trendy place, folks like us, though those guys being twins and quite large, something odd, different about them their bonhomie can't disguise.

SHAPE THE WORLD IS IN

in the secret heart of every
secret heart a secret heart lies broken

What is the shape of the unknown world surrounding me. Surrounding us. An empty question no doubt, as certain sets in logic are said to be empty. If a world is not known, how would anyone recognize its shape, even if they happened to catch a glimpse. Some people put faces on their gods or give their gods names and intelligible languages. I'm smart enough to know better, but ask my unanswerable question anyway. What surrounds me. How does it shape my beginning and end. The question worries me. I can't help asking it.

Especially early in the morning—five, six A.M.—and I'm on the toilet and sounds drift up. Through the plumbing, I suppose. Distant, quiet sounds that are also eerily close and intimate. My ears magnify what they hear. Like telescopes produce close-ups of the moon, planets, stars. Like binoculars reveal secrets inside a neighbor's window. Sounds shrinking distance. Empowering me. But if the sounds are far away, they cannot be as close as they seem. Am I hearing sounds inside or outside. Is there any way to tell whether something's truly out there or only here, inside me. Or both. Or nowhere. Listening, speculating doesn't get me closer to knowing. Maybe I'm peering through a telescope's wrong end or looking ass-backwards through binoculars I've reversed.

On mornings like this one, as I attempt to make sense of what I'm hearing, I feel myself getting smaller and smaller. As if I'm disappearing. Once I'm totally out of the way, perhaps sounds will clarify the world's shape. Transform me the way sound's magic turns noise to music. I'll be transparent to myself. Present and absent as I listen. Hear answers to an unanswerable question. Wait and listen. Listen and wait. Abuse sounds the way some people abuse drugs and alcohol. You understand what I mean, don't you. I use these early-morning sounds to forget who I am while I'm listening. Like the word *race* abused by a person who wants to forget another person's a human being.

Bathroom sounds of bathing in a tub. Am I here or there. Or two places at once. Mother and son sounds. Her washing him. Is that what I'm hearing. Although son large enough now to bathe mother. If it's them, they are two members of a family of three. Fellow tenants I've often observed going up and coming down in the elevator, though over all the years I've resided here, I've never seen the three of them together. Father a large, somewhat hulking retired cop. Dark-brown man, shy, with a limp. Maybe on a disability pension. Was he wounded on duty. Son visibly slow. Mother's color makes them a mixed couple, and son resembles neither mom nor pop. Adopted maybe. Or child of previous marriage. A boy who's the size of a smallish young man now. Old enough to grow a tribe of black hairs above his severely everted upper lip. He resembles mostly himself now.

With hints of that genetic clan likeness that identifies Down syndrome kids.

Who is doing what to whom down below. And what is the shape of the universe that begins foreign and unknown just beneath my feet beyond the onionskin of floor required to separate stories of a New York City high-rise co-op. Phantom flushes in the quiet, then silence, a faint roar echoing in the pipes while a shower runs, then more silence, and once in a great while voices, a cough, sigh, grunt, an irritated exclamation, silence again until a mother hums a lullaby or do I hear soft, singsong crooning of a boy caressed, tickled, soothed as he sinks deeper into a tubful of warm water, head tilted backward till he's almost submerged. Does she warn him, careful, careful, you'll get soapsuds in your eyes, soap she rubs into a lather on short arms, short legs he pokes out of the water and wiggles for her and then again and again, silence again, quiet, nothing but guesses most mornings, silent like when it's the father of the family's turn to lifeguard, hunkered down on a toilet probably directly below mine while I sit and daydream a boy who's almost near enough to touch and far away as a siren wailing in the city streets or earthquake in Guatemala or firestorms raging on a sun in another galaxy as it's consumed by a black hole whose birth I had followed on an iPad video simulation and recalled one morning squatting, waiting for my bowels to let go.

Same questions about the shape of the world I used to ask when a teacher, Mrs. Cosa, stood behind her desk writing on the blackboard. Asked myself, not her. She was too far away to ask. Her world no less mysterious, no less confusing to me than mine.

She was peculiarly detached. *Disembodied* is a word I could have used to describe Mrs. Cosa if I knew that word back then. My teacher at the board chalking words. Rules the class should copy into workbooks and memorize and be prepared to repeat on demand forever. Passing on these necessary words and rules happens to be her job, and she transmits them to us. Not responsible for words or rules any more than we are—they are not her, not hers—she probably learned them in a fashion similar to how we learn them, and wherever she lives when she leaves the classroom, she may obey or employ them or not, and there she may or may not pass them on to others, just as we are supposed to pass them on where we live, probably.

Words and rules here and she's not here, is what I thought. She's just up there—teacher not person—and we're just kids, not people either, her captive audience, and we aren't supposed to notice or be distracted by her body, history, identity, her personality in a classroom quiet as a grave except for taps and scratches of her writing on the blackboard. She's nobody in particular. Anonymous as a cop with a bullhorn blasting orders to an unruly crowd.

Her back mostly turned to us, Mrs. Cosa speaks over her shoulder in a manner that conveys nothing about herself, about us, except her tone of voice makes it clear she is not herself, not anyone, nor are we. We understand we must not miss the information her words are imparting, because without it we would certainly be less than the little we are, and we are nothing really anyway, nor is she. No matter how she's dressed, her age, size, years of teaching experience, it's not about her. Or us. Only rules, words on the blackboard count, her voice informs us. They count and belong to a larger, more significant world, basically inaccessible to her or to us. The importance of that other world apparent as it materializes in words she recites and inscribes on the board. Even our small minds can grasp the difference between that other place and this makeshift classroom where we have turned up to be exposed to something greater than we are or anything we might imagine on our own.

Rules and words incontestably not us, and for that reason we're correct to ignore her, the teacher, and ignore ourselves, a group of students incontestably not present, though here we are, too, and we better take down in our workbooks the rules, words she doesn't exactly fling over her shoulder or sprinkle like a farm lady feeding chickens. But we ought to be grateful as chickens. Our lives at risk, at stake if we don't pay attention or even if we do. We better gobble up what little we can of those words and rules to guide us in a dangerous, unforgiving world we will occasionally awaken from sleep to find ourselves immersed in, surrounded by.

In the morning, eavesdropping on sounds that drift up through the floor, occasionally I hear a radio or TV playing somewhere, in an empty room I believe, nobody listening to an announcer's voice all business, articulating snippets of news that fade, dissolve before I'm able to identify a single word, and I regret I didn't flat-out ask Mrs. Cosa the shape of the world.

Of course, no fourth-grade teacher, then or now, could answer my questions about where or how an unknowable world begins or ends. I don't blame Mrs. Cosa, even feel sorry for her. Not her fault I kept my question inside myself. Big crush on her once, piece of chalk in her hand, a small, neat, pale white lady all alone up there in front of us in her cat-eye glasses. Then again I'd get furious with her for reminding me we were all of us, teacher, room, school, hopelessly lost. Nowhere in fact. She's a turd, a stinking, ugly speck of shit floating around on the back of a roach with us till we all fall off again and land deeper in mucky nowhere.

If Mrs. Cosa heard me think that, I don't believe she'd be angry or hurt or insulted. She might even nod, Yes. Yes, but she's not responsible for what she is, is she. Doesn't know, does she. She's just there where she is. Like us in our seats or desks or boxes or emptified heads. Somebody else or some giant animal maybe squatted and pooped us, pooped her in front of us so don't ask. She didn't do it. Doesn't, couldn't know the answer. Words and rules not her, not hers. You shitty kids, what she would probably think or say about us if her mind were not busy performing this part of the job she's paid for. Rules. Words. And we'd probably agree. You're right, Mrs. Cosa. *Yes. Yes*, a pipey chorus of kid voices.

Reading a story or writing one, I hope the world will be different at the point the story ends. Same wish that motivates me some mornings to sit in the bathroom and listen for sounds, for silences telling me I am not the silence that surrounds me. Signs that assure me I possess a shape that belongs to me, and it can poke its way through silence, get on with a life. A different life I can't imagine. Except as difference. Except as unknowable.

World I want to be different is not like fictions stirred up by words on a page, not one that starts where its words start and finishes with the last word like any story I can choose to read or not or stop reading or stop writing and do my time elsewhere. The different world I long to inhabit is the one inhabiting me, no beginning or end. This world where I'm stuck forever, however long that might be. Me and everything else and nothing. Same space, same shape, same thing I am.

So I wait. And wait and listen and wait while the unknown drips somewhere, drop by drop like a leaky faucet in a bathroom I almost can hear from mine. Dripping drops of it accumulating in a sink until the sink overflows, and a flood faster than the speed of light takes everything with it wherever it goes to vanish. No mess left behind for anybody to clean up, no stories with a person inside waiting.

MY DEAD

Edgar Lawson Wideman: sept 2, 1918–dec 14, 2001
Bette Alfreda French Wideman: may 15, 1921–feb 7, 2008
Otis Eugene Wideman: march 6, 1945–jan 11, 2009
David Lawson Wideman: may 7, 1949–oct 19, 2014
Monique Renee Walters: nov 21, 1966–feb 6, 2015

I list my dead. Father. Mother. Brother. Brother. Sister's daughter. For some reason their funeral programs share a manila folder. During a bad ten months I had lost a brother, a niece, and they joined the rest of my dead. The dead remembered, forgotten, adrift. The dead in a folder. There and not here. Dead whose names never change. The dead who return secretly, anonymously, hidden within other names until they vanish, appear again.

March 6, the date I noted in my journal after I had compiled a list and returned the programs to their folder, happens to be my brother Otis Eugene's birthday, a date like others in the list, I tend to forget, as he is often forgotten when I revisit family memories. My younger brother Otis who survived our unforgettable mother barely a year. My quiet, forgettable brother, his birth separated from mine by four years, by twins, a boy and girl, neither living longer than a week.

Their deaths, of course, a terrible blow for our mother. She never spoke of those lost babies, and late in her life denied to my sister that the births had occurred. No dead twins in the four-year interval between me, her eldest, and my next brother, Otis. Other siblings arrived after the empty four years. New lives, two years separating each birth from the next, regular as rain, until five of us, four boys, one girl in the middle. With her hands full, heart full of caring for the ones alive, why would my mother allow herself to sink back into that abyss of watching two infants, so perfectly formed, so freshly dropped from inside her, leave the world and disappear as if her womb harbored death as naturally as life.

My brother was named Otis for our mother's brother and Eugene for our father's brother. Uncle Otis was very much alive, but Uncle Eugene dead already or soon to die on Guam, when my brother born. Uncle Eugene dying needlessly, or, you could say, ironically, since war with Japan officially declared over, a truce in force the sniper who shot Eugene didn't know about or perhaps refused to honor because too much killing, too many comrades dead. Why not shoot one more American soldier beachcombing for souvenirs where he had no right to trespass, no palpable reason to continue to live in the mind of an enemy whose duty was to repel invaders, to follow in his rifle's scope their movements. Not exactly easy targets, but almost a sure thing for a practiced marksman, even a sniper very weary, beat-up from no sleep, constant harassment of enemy planes, tanks, flamethrowers, a shooter trained to take his time, forget hunger, thirst, his dead, his home islands far too close to this doomed Guam as he gauges, tracks his prey, picks out a brown man who will surely, fatally fall before the others scatter for cover, before he, himself, is observed or snipered on this day he's not aware the war's over or is aware and doesn't care as he chooses someone to kill, freezes the rifle's swing, stops breathing, squeezes the trigger.

Uncle Otis, like our father and our father's brother, Eugene, served in World War II. Uncle Otis returned home to become a part of family life, always around until I was grown up with kids and my youngest sibling a teenager. We all still remember him fondly, Big Ote to distinguish him from Little Ote, my brother, who also carried the name of the uncle none of us in my generation had ever seen. Except I claimed to recall my uncle Eugene, even though my mother insistently objected, *no-no-no* you were way too young, just a baby when he left for the war. I persisted in my claim, wrote my first published story to bear witness to his living presence within me, my closeness with a long-dead man more intimate, continuous, and attested, I'm almost ashamed to admit, than recollections I have of his namesake, my brother. A brother who, for reasons never shared with me, preferred to be called Gene once he became an adult.

Gene, the name everybody I met in Atlanta called him when I traveled there for his funeral. Over the years I had taught myself to say *Gene* when I addressed my brother in groups not family or introduced him to strangers or on those rare occasions when just the two of us were conversing and I wanted to show him I treated his wish to be called Gene seriously, how once, anyway, in this specific case I would make an effort to forget I was his elder, oldest of the siblings, and follow his lead. Act as if his right to name himself might really matter to me, and for once he could set the rules. My little brother Gene in charge, and me behaving as if he has escaped the box, the traps I spent so much evil time elaborately, indefatigably laying for him during our childhood. Not much use for a younger brother when we were growing up. Except when he served as temporary or potential victim and I was, yes, yes, like some goddamned sniper drawing a bead on an enemy soldier totally unaware his life dangled at the end of a thread in my fingers.

Gene. In Atlanta the name didn't sound like the affectation I had once considered it, my brother's rather late in the day, thus partly funny, partly irrelevant and futile striking out for independence. An attempt perhaps to wipe the slate clean by rebaptizing himself and answering only to a name he had chosen. A not-too-subtle effort to cancel prerogatives and status other members of the family had earned over the long haul of growing up intertwined, separate and unequal. Like the privilege I had granted myself, no blame or guilt attached, to seldom phone him. To not recall or acknowledge him whatsoever for long stretches of time if I chose. My forgettable brother.

Now I concede it was less a matter of qualities he possessed or didn't possess that caused him to be forgettable, but my presumptions, my bottomless unease. Wasn't I the most worthy, important brother in the family, the world. The one who, therefore, must occupy all space available, even if no space left for anyone else. Forgetting a brother a convenient tactic to ensure I never found him in my way. An annoyance. A barrier. A ghost.

I went to Atlanta to bury a brother and found Gene. Not Otis or Little Ote. Not Otis Eugene. Once my brother chose Gene as his new name, I stopped associating that name with the uncle who had died in the Pacific war. Eugene whose big sneakers I believed I remembered seeing on live feet. People in Atlanta who knew my brother had probably never heard of Eugene, our dead uncle. When they talked about a Gene, the name transformed me into a stranger, an intruder. I recalled names I had made up to keep my brother in his place, tease him to tears in ugly games while we were kids stuck in the same small house. Names I'd forgotten after we both left home. Then for years and years almost no name necessary for him. Few occasions arose to speak of a brother or speak to him or summon him into my thoughts.

I could have let him be Gene in Atlanta. Isn't that what he asked. Wasn't that one reason for his long, self-imposed exile. No trips back home unless someone very sick, dying, dead. Another city, another state, another start with another name he had picked. A new family, not necessarily to replace the old but to fill emptiness where maybe he'd always felt homeless or smothered or locked down in spaces like the ones I allowed him. Spaces with room for him only if he stayed in them alone.

I could have let myself be satisfied with seeing Gene, convinced myself I was saying goodbye to a stranger in Atlanta, but it was him, his neat, pencil-thin mustache, elegant features, my brother's unbegrudging silence in the open casket.

MUSIC

I find my sister in the big, soft chair where I'd usually find Charles. Television playing with no sound. She is asleep until I pat her shoulder and her eyelids flutter. Leaning down closer to her ear I say, "Time for bed, miss."

She's dressed for bed. Probably had been upstairs to bed at least once before she wound up in the chair in front of a muted TV in the living room at three in the morning where I had wandered after bed and sleep failed me, too.

As I had tipped down the dark stairs, blinks of light from the living room did not help much, and my hand used the wooden banister on the stairwell's open side to guide me, to remind me that a rail laid atop the steps ran down along the opposite wall, a steel track for an incline that carried a chair up and down, a rail that could trip you up and break your neck if you weren't careful.

"Dreamed of my girl," my sister, eyes shut again, halfway whispers as if worried speaking too loud might disturb somebody's sleep. Her own. Her dream.

Dreaming of a daughter who had died only a few months before this visit, whose long illness had confined her to a wheelchair that required the motorized lift I'd just been avoiding. This is what I think first when I hear my sister's words, but something soft in her voice had opened to let me enter, and I understand the girl she dreamed of was two girls, my grown-up niece whose untouched room I'm not yet prepared to enter alone, and the baby, not quite two, lost how many, many years ago, and as usual when I recall the one who never grew up, always strangely older and younger than her sister, a song starts to play, silently as pictures moving across the screen until I turn off the TV. That old Spinners song we had danced to in this same room, dark then, too. My niece tiny, fever sweaty, swaddled in a nightgown, me cradling her in my arms, blowing on her brow to cool it with my breath as we swayed, near to sleep like my sister in the chair who bestirs herself, reaches back to plant her palms on the armrests, scrunches her weight forward to get it balanced on her feet to stand. To smile, to go up to bed.

BONDS

She struggles to keep him inside her. Not because she knows that in less than six months Japan will bomb Pearl Harbor and this country, flags flying, will join in the slaughter of world war and that child after child, all colors, sizes, shapes, religions, nationalities, including babies like the one she's expecting, will be gathered up and starved, tortured, incinerated.

Struggles to keep her baby inside not because she understood the horror of war, understood that once it starts the horror never ends, young men put in uniforms and marched off to save the country or die trying, some of those soldiers young men from her colored neighborhood, two she will never meet except as names on a memorial plaque beside the door of Homewood's Carnegie public library, where her brother Otis, who made it back from war, used to take her by the hand to borrow books, then years later took her son, men returning she will encounter in the street or in movies or on TV, some full of love for any girl or boy inside her, men who gladly would risk their lives to protect her or her children playing in the streets, but others rotten with war's hate, men with weapons the government issues and teaches them to shoot, men who would kill, no regrets, any children she'd bear.

She struggles to keep the baby inside not because she feared terrible pain once she starts to squeeze him out. Pain scalding her they say worse than the hot comb when her mother digs too deep. *Told you stop your fidgeting, girl. Holler and jump you make me burn you again.* She'd never disbelieved the women's stories about how godawful the pain. Harder to believe what they said about how suddenly easy it is afterwards, after all the suffering, your insides tearing apart inch by inch, then out comes the baby and it's a sweet, warm bundle on your chest and you won't remember why all the screams and carrying-on. Won't remember you'd been thinking just minutes before you'd rather die than burn one second more.

She keeps him inside not because she knew the baby a *he*, not because she knew she'd be closer to the end of her life once his life begins. Not because she knew his eyes the last eyes to see her alive. Him silent on a hospital chair beside her hospital bed, book in his hands, monitor beep-beep-beeping, his eyes on a page the precise instant she's no more, missing her last breath.

She's determined to keep the baby inside longer not because longer might change the baby's color or keep money always in her child's pocket. Longer inside not because of things she knows or should or could or might not want to know. She holds him inside because she's sure the day is Friday, June thirteen, and sure the child she carries already has two strikes against it—strike of poor, strike of colored—and no way she's going to let a third strike—

bad luck of being born on Friday the thirteenth—doom every day of her first child's life on earth before it even gets here.

She will struggle till midnight. Then four or five minutes past midnight, she decides. For good measure. To be absolutely certain. Four or five minutes more of agony, bearable or not bearable.

Then okay . . . *okay now*, she will say to herself, no strength left to speak the words aloud. No one in the room but her anyway, so she thinks *okay.* Rolls her eyeballs up to the wall clock to be sure, an effort that almost kills her, and then *okay now*, she says. Lets go of all that scorching air hoarded inside her gut. Only a tiny hole for it to pass through. She gasps, hollers. Sighs and gulps. A dull pop then a pop-popping push, rush, and *shit . . . oh, shit.* Please, not shit. Let it be air, a fart, no, many rumbling humongous farts. And *oh my, oh my, my* she's spewing water, blood, beans, those baked beans doctor and mother both had warned her not to eat. Beans, a baby, a nasty mess dirtying the bed, cleaning out her insides. A small voice in her head mutters feeble apologies, but she knows she's smiling. Stinky. Wet. Warm. Not alone.

She struggled to hold him inside a little longer she tells him one day because on that miserable night of June 13, and with two strikes against him she had no power to change, she told herself to stop shuddering, squirming, moaning, and groaning. Wrapped herself in bonds of steel. Steel around thighs, knees. Steel tying her ankle bones together so no part of him leaks or peeks or sneaks out and gets struck by a bolt of Friday the Thirteenth's evil lightning.

* * *

She struggled to keep the baby inside not because she feared losing her first one. Not because she feared it might be her last. Not because she understood what would happen or not happen to the boy or girl. She held on because six minutes of June 14, 1941, needed to pass before she'd let go, and now more than three-quarters of a century has passed, many, many June fourteens, and each one his birthday, him alive and breathing and her, too, he tells her, and won't let go.

NEW START

We were in bed watching TV. My beautiful, scared wife and scared, colored me. Watching had become our nightly habit since treatments began that might save my life if they didn't kill me. We'd pick a series recommended by somebody we liked, with, ideally, lots of seasons already under its belt, so depending on mood, degree of exhaustion, length and quality of episodes, we could choose to watch one, two, sometimes, rarely, three before sleep. Or watch, as was often the case, before a night of broken sleep. Restless, anxious. Waiting for morning. One day less in the countdown to my final treatment. One night less. Us closer to the next night we could start to watch again.

In one of Downton Abbey's cavernous rooms, large enough to hold the entire house I grew up in, a room whose art and furnishings worth more money than you'd need to pay off all mortgages on every dwelling in the block of real estate in Pittsburgh, Pennsylvania, where my family had lived, the Abbey's owners and present residents sit and stand, posed elegantly, drinks in hand or close enough at hand to reach easily or to be handed to them by an efficient servant. A cast of meticulously dressed and groomed

British aristocrats exhausted, a bit stunned by the financial success, announced only moments before, of the tour of Downton some of them had just finished conducting, ushering members of the public, willing to pay, through fabled inner sanctums of their ancestral home in order to raise funds for a war memorial to honor young men of the village who had gone off to fight the Kaiser's legions and would never return.

So many visitors. So many strangers willing to buy a ticket. Such curiosity. The interest not unexpected, of course. Downton Abbey was Downton Abbey, wasn't it. And always would be, would it not, thank you. Thank goodness. Long lines all afternoon. The endless questions. Adult villagers, farmers, laborers, tradespeople wide-eyed as children stringing along beside and behind them, even people in service at other Great Houses streaming in, excited, cowed to speechlessness at certain moments, faces expressing awe or almost reverence of a sort. Like peasants in church. Or country folk at a traveling carnival delighted by an opportunity to be delighted, or delighted by the privilege of a few hours free to play at being delighted. A public, private treat. Or even treatment, you might call it. Church on Sunday morning. A day at a country fair. A slow amble through polished marvels of Downton Abbey led by one of its formidable denizens.

And, wasn't that it. Wasn't a guide, one of us close enough to touch, the touch that made a tour inside Downton utterly unforgettable for the dears.

No. No-no, Cousin. They flock to view us in our cages. A day at the zoological gardens to observe odd creatures through the bars.

* * *

What a perfectly disagreeable idea. Shame on you, you wicked girl. Surely you don't believe that our *guests* entertain actual thoughts. Goodness gracious, dear. Why bother ourselves one tad about that lot or their notions. Except to recall that Mr. Branson reported money positively poured in today. More tours could produce useful revenue.

More tours. No-no-no. Please. Never again. Heavens, no . . .

In bed we watch and listen. Tourists, too. Paying, too. Watch a moment in a TV melodrama when a tour conducted by Downton Abbey's owners surprises them into a sudden awareness of themselves as characters in a show being staged for an audience, watched by an audience. A moment characters did not see coming until the script demands a tour of their imaginary lives.

Downton Abbey's characters slightly dismayed when they realize the roles they play consume, not save them. A show may be a long-running hit, yet remains temporary. Empires fall, individual lives, virtuous or villainous, collapse. Sooner or later, no matter how convincingly an actor renders a character, you can only fool some of the people some of the time. And even though a sucker born every minute and fools rush in and writers contrive sudden, unexpected exits and entrances to unsettle or entice viewers, everybody knows that sooner or later, all good things must come to an end.

After the scene I'm recalling, after tours had been dispensed at Downton Abbey and crowds had passed from room to room, all visitors finally led away, gate locked, big day over, we watch till the episode concludes. Reach this last room. Last scene. Just the two of us, alone, quiet, TV dark, watching ourselves watch an empty screen. Stuck here frightened in our bed. Tour dissolving and we have nowhere else to go. I try to imagine someone watching us, watching through eyes not ours, eyes present, attentive. We need eyes to watch us. Watching as if we are special and eternal as nobility. Eyes that imagine the show we perform worth more of their time.

To feel safe again we need others spying on us as we spy on them, their eyes a video cam that hovers above us all in the sky. But the same camera delivering us to others and delivering them to us delivers other shows, many shows, far too many, all beamed at once—floods, fires, earthquakes, plagues of incurable disease, young men in antique uniforms exploded to gravy just yesterday in the bottom of trenches in France, a brown young man slumped today in the front seat of a Honda Civic, bloody, dying, dead. Woman narrating the story we observe as it unfolds, her voice-over oddly detached until it breaks, *Don't tell me you shot him, Officer, please don't tell me you shot my man—bang, bang, bang, bang—four times—don't tell me my love's dead, Officer, please, sir, don't say it.*

Shows intervene and we can't turn them off, competing, multiplying, streaming faster than the speed of light on millions of screens.

I think I hear the Downton actors complain, Stop watching us, please. Stop watching, waiting to see us lose our places, our lives. Watching us to forget who you are. Watching us undress, watching us weep. Crying along with us. As if you don't dance, pray, burn, too. As if you don't pretend to be real. Stop, please. Allow us to do our jobs. Maintain our distance, composure. Our characters. Please. Go your way and let us go ours. Why would you wish to see us as we see you, dead on an empty screen.

I recite to myself the simple rules. How we arrive here, empty-handed, and must stand in line for tickets, rain or shine. How all stories are true, my love, like ours, until we tumble out of them and then they are different and true again. How we are required to stand in drizzle outside the Abbey's gate. Silence the rule until the show starts again. Silence the rule while we imagine treats wonderful as the promise of blue skies over our heads, wonderful as a time when anyone can be king or queen for a day.

No TV. Room dark. Are we closer to sleep or no sleep. Man and wife, each of us alone now. Scared woman, scared man. Wondering what comes next. Our bedroom like a space where people stand before a movie starts or the space where you hover in a restaurant until a table cleared for your meal. I think of the little plaque almost hidden in a corner by subtle lighting in Clandestino, our favorite chic but not too expensive Lower East Side spot. *If waiters could talk.*

MAPS AND LEDGERS

My first year teaching at the university my father killed a man. I'm ashamed to say I don't remember the man's name, though I recall the man a good buddy of my father and they worked for the city of Pittsburgh on a garbage truck and the man's family knew ours and we knew some of them, my sister said. Knew them in that way black people who lived in the same neighborhood knew each other and everybody else black in a city that divided itself by keeping all people of color in the same place back then no matter where in the city you lived.

I did not slip up, say or do the wrong thing when the call that came into the English Department, through the secretary's phone to the chairman's phone, finally reached me, after the secretary had knocked and escorted me down the hall to the chair's office, where I heard my mother crying because my father in jail for killing a man and she didn't know what to do except she had to let me know. She knew I needed to know and knew no matter how much a call would upset me, I would be more upset if she didn't call, even though calling meant, since I didn't have a home phone yet nor a direct line in my office and no cell phones, she would have to use the only number I'd given her and said to use only for emergencies and wasn't this an emergency, hers, mine, we had to deal with, she and I, her trying not to weep into the phone she was holding in Pittsburgh while she spoke to strangers in Philadelphia, white people strangers to make it worse, a woman's voice then a man's before she reached me with the news I needed to know and none of it anybody's business, terrible business breaking her heart to say to me even though I needed to know and would want to know despite where I was and who I was attempting to be, far away from home, surrounded by strangers probably all of them white which made everything worse she didn't need to say because I heard it in her voice by the fifth or sixth word, her voice that didn't belong in the chair's office, a story not for a chairperson's ears, but he was southern gentleman enough as well as enough of a world-renowned Chaucer scholar to hand me the phone and excuse himself and shut the office door behind him so I could listen in peace to my mother crying softly and trying to make sense of a dead man and my father in jail for killing him, his cut-buddy I can say to myself now and almost smile at misunderstandings, bad jokes, ill will, superiority, inferiority stirred up when I switch between two languages, languages almost but never quite mutually intelligible, one kind I talked at home when nearly always only colored folks listening, another kind spoken and written by white folks talking to no one or to one another or at us if they wanted something from us, two related-by-blood languages that throttled or erased or laughed at or disrespected each other more often than engaging in useful exchange, but I didn't slip once in my conversation with the chair, didn't say my gotdam daddy cut his gotdamn cut-buddy, no colored talk or nigger jokes from either of us in the office when a phone call from my mom busted in and blew away my cover that second or third day of my first or second week of my first college teaching job.

My aunt C got my father a lawyer. Aunt C lived five doors away on our street, Copeland, when I was growing up. My family of Mom, Dad, five kids had moved into an upstairs three-room apartment in a row house at the end of a block where a few colored families permitted because the housing stock badly deteriorated and nobody white who could afford not to wanted to live on the busted block, after coloreds had been sneaked into a few of Copeland's row houses or modest two-story dwellings squeezed in between, like the one Aunt C and her husband could afford to buy and fix up because he was a numbers banker, but most of us coloreds, including my mother and father, had to scrimp and scuffle just to occupy month by month, poaching till the rent man put us out in the street again, but residents long enough for their kids to benefit for a while from better schools of a neighborhood all white except for a handful of us scattered here and there down at the bottom of a couple streets like Copeland.

Aunt C a rarity, a pioneer you might say because she worked in the planning office of the city, a good job she finessed, she explained to me once, by routing her application through the Veterans Administration since she'd served as a WAC officer during WW II and guessed that by the time the city paper pushers noticed her color disqualified her, the military service record that made her eligible for a position and elevated her to the top of the list would have already gotten her hired, only woman, only colored, decades before anybody colored not a janitor or cleaning woman got hired by the city to work in downtown office buildings. Aunt C who I could always count on to find some trifling job around her house for me to earn a couple quarters when I needed pocket change or bigger jobs car washing, neatening up and cutting the grass in her tiny backyard when I needed new sneakers or a new shirt my parents couldn't buy, and then counted on her again years later because she was the one who knew everybody and everybody's dirt downtown, and got my father—her elder brother—an attorney, a colored one who also knew everybody and everybody's dirt downtown, the man as much or more of a rarity, an exception in his way as my aunt since he not only practiced law but served in the state legislature as majority speaker, an honor, achievement, irony, and incongruity I haven't been able to account for to this day, but he wound up representing my father and saving him from prison, thanks to Aunt C. That same colored lawyer one day would say to me, shaking his head and reaching out and placing his hand on my shoulder, *Family of poor old Aeschylus got nothing on yours, son*, as if to inform me, though he understood both of us already knew, that once my mother's phone call had caught up with me, Aunt C doing her best or no Aunt C—things would only get worse.

No, my father didn't serve time for murder. Lawyer plea-bargained self-defense and victim colored like my father anyway so they chose to let my father go. But things did get worse. My father's son, my youngest brother, convicted of felony murder. And years later my son received a life sentence at sixteen. My brother, my son still doing time. And my father's imprisoned son's son a murder victim. And a son of my brother's dead son just released from prison a week ago. And I'm more than half ashamed I don't know if the son, whose name I can't recall, of my brother's dead son has fathered a son or a daughter. My guess is the rumor of a child true since if my grandnephew was old enough for adult prison, he would be way past the age many young colored men father babies back home.

Gets confusing doesn't it. Precedents from Greek mythology or not. Knowing or not knowing what variety of worse will probably come next if you are a member of my colored family hunkering down at the end of Copeland or on whatever divided street you think of as home or whatever you may think a home is. Gets damned confusing. I lose track of names. Generations. No end in sight. Or maybe I already know the end and just don't want to think about it out loud. Whose gotdam business is it anyway. Knucklehead, fucking hardhead youngbloods and brothers. Gotdamned Daddy. Gotdamned cut-buddy. Words I didn't slip and say out loud that day attempting to explicate an emergency to my chairman in the departmental office.

Get away, I kept telling myself, and none of this happens.

I always had been impressed by my grandmother Martha's beautiful hand. Not her flesh-and-blood hand. Her letters. Her writing. Perfect letter after letter in church ledgers and notebooks year after year in my grandmother Martha's beautiful hand. You almost felt a firm, strong hand enfolding, guiding yours if your turn to read Sunday school attendance or minutes of the Junior Deacons' board, each letter flowing into the next into the next word then next sentence so you didn't stumble or mumble repeating aloud what you found waiting for you so peacefully, patiently, perfectly shaped between faint blue lines on each page. Not that her hands weren't hands a person might notice and think something nice about. Maybe a bit mannishly large but my grandmother Martha wasn't a small woman, her wide-boned hips not swaying side to side when she walked, more of a tall person's rocking-chair lean and tipping-forward-then-back momentum that propelled her strides, striding down the sidewalk purposefully though never in a hurry, walking like you'd probably imagine she probably writes when she records church business, her hand's fingers slim, smooth-jointed, tapering to big teardrop nails she often painted plum to complement light brown skin.

Letter after letter perfect as eggs. Perfect as print. But better. Her hand cursive. Letters flow like alive things that grow. One growing live into or from the other whether connections visible or not. As the Bible grows if you are taught to read it in the fashion I was. Each verse, each psalm, parable, book, sermon connected. Truths alive and growing in the pages after you learn in church how to read Bible words. Cursive you learn in school. *Cursive* one of many strange words telling you a different language spoken in school and you will always be a stranger in that strange land. Not everybody good at cursive, not every boy or girl in class remembers new words, nor gives a flying fuck if they do or don't, but my grandmother's cursive flows seamlessly page after page when you leaf through one of the old Homewood AME Zion notebooks and ledgers with thick, ornate covers she filled and you are not aware until you discover one more time as you always do how shabby the world will be, how much it hurts when her hand drops yours and perfect writing stops.

My grandmother picked her husbands as carefully, perfectly as she performed her church secretary cursive. Except every now and then she decided it was time to change scripts. After she abandoned then divorced her first husband—a dark-skinned workingman, shy emigrant from rural Promised Land, South Carolina, father of my father and my aunt C, the man I grew up calling Grandpa—my grandmother Martha chose to marry preachers. A series of three or four preachers whose names I often could not remember when they were alive, names mostly lost now they are dead, like the name of the man my father killed. Uncle this or Uncle that is what I called my grandmother's husbands and one I called "Reverend" because he addressed me as "Professor," a darkie joke we shared, minstrels puffing each other up with entitles, *Yo, Mr. Bones . . . Wuss up, Mr. Sambo.*

Same grandmother who wrote beautiful cursive played deaf (almost but not quite her version of darkie joke) when people were saying things she preferred not to hear. A highly selective deficit she displayed only when she chose. For instance, sitting on her pink couch she protected with a transparent plastic slip-cover, chattering away with a roomful of other family members, if someone mentioned the name of one of ours in trouble or prison, my grandmother Martha would shut her eyes, duck her head shyly, totally absent herself as if she'd suddenly nodded off like very old folks do. If you didn't know better, you'd think she was missing the conversation. Elsewhere. Immune. But if the unpleasant topic not dropped quickly enough to suit her, she would shush the person speaking by tapping an index finger against her pursed lips. *Not nice . . . Shhhh.* Some mean somebody might be listening and spread nasty news about a son or grandson or nephew shot dead in the street three years ago or locked up in the pokey twenty years, or a slave two hundred years ago. *Shhhh.* Whisper, she orders as she leans over, pouts, and mimics whispering. Best whisper in a family member's ear so cruel strangers can't overhear, can't mock names of our dead, our wounded, our missing ones.

I regard my empire. Map it. Set down its history in ledgers. Envy my grandmother's beautiful hand. Her cold-bloodedness. I've done what I needed to do to get by, and when I look back, the only way to make sense of my actions is to tell myself that at the time it must have seemed I had no other choice.

As far back as I can remember, I was aware the empire I was building lived within an empire ruled by and run for the benefit of a group to which I did not belong. *Mm'fukkahs, the man, honkies, whitey, boss, peckerwoods, mam, fools, mister, sir, niggas* some of the names we used for this group not us, and the list of names I learned goes on and on, as many names probably as *they* learned to call us by. Growing up, if I found myself talking to people, small gathering or large, almost always it would be composed exclusively of members of my group or, except for me, members of the other. On the other hand nothing unusual about contact between the two groups. Ordinary, daily mixing the rule not exception. In public spaces we politely ignored each other or smiled or evaded or bumped, jostled, violently collided, or clashed. Passed through each other as easy as stepping through a ghost. Despised, killed each other just as easily, though since the others held the power, many, many more fatal casualties in our group resulting from those encounters than in theirs.

Majority rules, we learned. Fair enough. Except, since we spent most of our time among our own kind talking, interacting only with each other, slippage occurred naturally. Reinforced by the presence of friends and family, we considered ourselves among ourselves the equal of others. Or considered ourselves better. Considered our status as minority, as inferior not to be facts. Or at best relative facts, irrelevant to us unless we assumed the point of view of the group not our group. On good days members of our group would make fun of such an assumption. Bad-mouth the other group with all the nasty names we dreamt up for them. Names and laughter like talismans—string of garlic, sign of the cross—European people in the old days would brandish to fend off a vampire. A survival strategy we practiced while the other group survived by arming themselves, by erecting walls, prisons, churches, laws. By chanting, screaming, repeating, believing their words for us.

Ain't nothing but a party, old Aunt May always said. How long, how long, sighed Reverend Felder, in Homewood AME Zion's pulpit, Dr. King in Atlanta's Ebenezer Baptist.

Aunt May's skin a lighter color than my grandmother Martha's light brown, and the difference, slight though it was, cowed my grandmother enough to look the other way or pretend to be deaf when May got loud, raunchy, or ignorant at family gatherings. May, tumbler of whiskey held down with one hand on the armrest pad of her wheelchair while the hand at the end of her other arm points, wiggles, summons all at once, a gesture synced with a holler, growl, and mm-mm, boy, you better get yourself over here and gimme some sugar, boy, get over here and dance with your aunt May, boy, you think you grown now, don't you, you sweetie pie, past dancing wit some old, crippled-up lady in a wheelchair, ain't that what you thinking, boy. Well, this old girl ain't done yet. Huh-uh. You all, hear me, don't, you. Ain't nothin but a party. Woo-wee. Get your narrow hips over here, you fine, young man, and dance wit May.

They left something behind in Aunt May's gut they shouldn't have when they sewed her up after surgery. Staple, piece of tape, maybe a whole damn scalpel my sister rolled her eyes telling me. You know how they do us, my sister said, specially old people can't help themselves, won't speak up—poor May in terrible pain, belly blew up and almost dead a week after they sent her home. So weak and full of drugs poor thing lying there in her bed could barely open her eyes. But you know Aunt May. Ain't going nowhere till she ready to go. Hospital didn't want her back, but we fussed till they sent an ambulance. Opened her up again and took out whatever festering. May got better. Didn't leave from here till she was good and ready to leave. You know May. Hospital assholes never even said they were sorry. Threw May away like a dirty old rag after they saw they hadn't quite killed her, and then got busy covering their tracks. May dead two years before anybody admitted any wrongdoing. Too late to hold the hospital accountable. Simple-minded as all those pale folks on May's side the family always been, couldn't get their act together and sue the doctors or hospital or some cotton-picking somebody while May still alive.

May's nephew, Clarence, you remember him. Browner than I am, I reminded my sister as if she didn't already know. I ran into him five, six years ago, when I was in town for something. Clarence a cook now. Guess at some point May and her pale sisters decided some color might be a good idea. Two, maybe three married brothers from the same brown-skinned family, didn't they, and broke the color line so Clarence and a bunch of our other second cousins or half cousins or whatever after a couple more generations of marrying and mixing got different colors and names and I've lost track, but Clarence I knew because he was my age and a Golden Gloves boxer and everybody knew him and knew his older brother, Arthur, in jail for bank robbing, put away big-time in a federal penitentiary, so when Clarencie walked into Mrs. Schaefer's eleventh-grade class, which was a couple grades further than Clarencie ever got, he wasn't supposed to be in that eleventh-grade classroom or any other, he just happened to be hanging out, strolling the high school halls and saw me and came in and hollered, Hey, Cuz, how you doing, man . . . and me, I kind of hiss-whispered back, Hey, what you doing here, him acting like nobody else in the classroom when he strutted in, walked straight to my seat in the back, loud-talking the whole way till I popped up, Hey, Cuz, and hugged him, shocking the shit out of Mrs. Schaefer because I was her nice boy, good student and good citizen and example for all the other hoodlums. You could tell how terrified the poor white lady was most the time, coming every day into a school not all colored yet but getting there and getting worse and she needed me as much as I needed her we both understood so who in hell was this other tall, colored boy acting like he owned her classroom with nobody he had to answer to but himself and that was my cousin Clarencie, he couldn't care less what anybody else thought, Cousin Clarence, and you could tell just looking at him once, stranger to you or not, that you better go on about your own business and hope this particular reddish-brown-skinned negro with straight, dago-black hair and crazy eyes got no business with you, you heard the stories didn't you, Sis. You most likely told some of them to me—bouncer at a club downtown, mob enforcer maybe, got paid for doing time for the crime of some mafia thug don and afterwards Cousin Clarence a kind of honorary made-man people say, but most of the worst of that bad stuff long after we hugged and grinned and took over Mrs. Schaefer's class a minute because he didn't care and I forgot for once to care whom it belonged to.

Aunt C, my father's sister, got him a fine lawyer. But things continued to get worse. Worse is what you begin to expect if worse is what you get time after time. Worse, worser, worst. Don't let the ugly take you down, my mother said. Don't let it make you bitter and ugly, she said. She had led me by the hand to a few decent places inside me where she believed and tried to convince me that little sputtering lights would always exist to guide how I should behave once I left home and started a grown-up life. Her hand not as powerful and elegant as my grandmother Martha's, but my mother wrote good letters, clear, to the point, often funny, her cursive retaining features of the young girl she'd been when she learned to write. Neat, precise, demonstrating obviously she'd been an attentive student, yearned to get right the lessons she was taught.

Earnest another way of putting it, *it* being my mom's character when she was a schoolgirl and then when she fell in love with my father, I bet, and that sort of mother, too, I absolutely know, serious, conscientious without being boring, never boring because whatever she undertook she performed in the spirit partly of girls in grade school nearly junior high age, always a little scared but bold, too, both idly mischievous and full of hidden purpose, full of giggles and iron courage adults could never comprehend, often dismiss, yet stand in awe also, charmed, protective of the spark, that desire of young colored girls to grow and thrive, their hunger to connect with an unknown world no matter how perilous that new-to-them world might turn out to be for girls determined to discover exciting uses for limbs, minds, hearts still forming, still as stunning for them to possess as those girl hearts, minds, limbs were stunning for adults to behold. In the case of my mother, from girlhood to womanhood, an infectious curiosity, a sense of not starting over but starting fresh, let's go here, let's do this, not because she had mastered a situation or a moment previously but because uncertainty attracted, motivated, formed her.

Look at this writing, I can almost hear her say, look at these letters, words, sentences, ideas, feelings that flow and connect when we attempt something in this particular, careful fashion, with this cursive we studied and repeated in a classroom, but mine now, see, see it going word by word, carefully, and I follow her words, her writing like that of a bright child's who is occasionally distracted while she busily inscribes line after almost perfect line from manual to copybook. Going the way it's supposed to go. And where it's going, nobody knows exactly where but it looks the way it should and worth the trouble, the practice, because it's mine now and yours, too, she tells me, if you wish, and work hard at it. Whatever. Take my hand. Hold it as I hold yours, precious boy, and let's see, let's see what we shall see.

That's the message I read in her hand, in letters my mother sent when I went away to college. Letters I receive today from home beyond these pages. Home we share with all our dead.

* * *

I thought at the time, the time when I'd just begun university teaching, that the worst consequence of my father stabbing another man to death would be my first meeting with the chair in his office after I returned from Pittsburgh. After I'd said to my mother, Don't worry, I'll be home soon, and hung up the phone and tried to explain an ugly, complicated situation in as few words as possible and the chair had generously excused me from my teaching duties and granted me unconditional license to attend to family affairs, *A terrible business. Sorry it hit before you could get yourself settled in here.* The worst would be wisdom, commiseration, condolences I'd have to endure one more time animating his face, in his office, in his position as departmental chair after I completed my dirty work at home and stood in his office again, forgiven again by his unrufflable righteousness.

A good man, my mother would call him. Ole peckerwood, May would say. I heard both voices, responded to neither. Too busy worrying about myself. Too confused, enraged, selfish. Not prepared yet to deal with matters far worse afflicting my father, his victim, the victim's family, all my people back home, our group that another more powerful group has treated like shit for centuries to intimidate and oppress, to prove to themselves that a country occupied by many groups belongs forever, solely, unconditionally to one group.

My sister needs a minute or so to summon up the name, but then she's certain, "James . . . and I think his first name Riley . . . uh-huh . . . Riley James . . ." she says is the name of the man our father killed. Neither of us speaks. Silence we both maintain for a while is proof probably she's correct. Silence of a search party standing at the edge of a vast lake after the guide who's led them to it points and says the missing one is out there somewhere. Silence because we've already plunged, already groping in the chill murkiness, holding our breath, dreading what we'll recover or not from the gray water.

Thought I'd recognize the name if I heard it. That jolt, you know, when you're reminded of something you will never forget. But James sounds right, anyway. And Riley James had kids, didn't he. Yes, my sister says. Three. One a girl about my age I'm pretty sure. Used to run into her before it happened.

Coming up, did you ever think we might need to have this conversation one day. Daddy killing someone else's daddy.

Oh, we knew. Children understand. Don't need adults to tell them certain things. Kids supposed to listen to grown-ups, better listen if you don't want a sore behind, but we watch them, too. Kids always watching, wondering why big people do what they do. Understand a whole lotta mess out there adults not talking about. Scary mess kids can't handle. Or maybe nobody kid or adult can handle it, so you better keep your eyes wide open. Don't even know what you looking for except it's bad. Gonna get you if you not careful. But no. Thank goodness, no. Huh-uh, I'm not standing here today saying that when I was a little girl I could see my father would kill another man. But we knew, we saw with our own eyes awful stuff happening day after day and worse just around the corner waiting to happen. Grown-ups didn't need to tell us all that mess happening to them. We watched while it happened.

Wish I could disagree, Tish. Wish I could say no, but no, I think we probably did know. You're remembering right again, my sweet lil sis.

Whoa. Don't remember everything, but some things I sure don't forget, so lighten up some on the sweet sister bullshit. As if you always treated me like I was your sweet lil sister. Like youall's favorite game back then wasn't teasing and beating on me to see me cry. My little brothers torturing me as soon as they were big enough. And you, too, eldest brother. They learned it from you. You . . . you not me always the sweet one. Oldest, sweetest one. At least that's what you had all the adults in the family calling you and believing about you. Him so nice. All those good grades in school and talks so nice to grown-up people, so smart and a good boy takes care of his little brothers and sister to help out his mother. What a sweet, nice boy. Wasn't hardly bout no sweet lil sis, you devil. My sweet eldest brother the king. Making me pay in spades if I dared to sass you or look at you cross-eyed or stick out my tongue or beg please, Mom, could I please have that last little wing, the wing you had your eye on since you sat down at the table and counted the pieces of chicken on the plate and figured an extra one left after everybody got their share and that extra wing meant for you.

Okay. Warm and safe and nice as we felt home was, maybe not always but lots of the time, really, still there was the worry about worse coming. Could hear it when Daddy slammed the door behind himself going out. Or I peeped at Mom's red eyes. Or checked out the thumb she chewed on. Or Daddy's clean, ironed white shirts he pitched in the laundry basket and wouldn't wear till they came back starched in cellophane wrappers from the cleaners. Or Mom forgets she's scrubbed a pot clean and stands at the kitchen sink humming gospel and scrubs and scrubs and scrubs.

Thinking now about Mom's poor thumb, didn't I suck on mine when I was a little girl. Yes indeed I did. Seems to me I recall you sneaking off when nobody paying attention and you sucking yours, too.

Yes, all that's so. Still, whether or not we knew things would get worse, our fear doesn't answer the question, why. You must wonder now like I do. Why. Why did things get worse.

Wish I knew the answer to that one, older brother.

Will it always be like this, then. Too late. Damage done. Another victim. Trial. Funeral. Inquest. Story in the newspaper, on TV. More tears. Hand-wringing.

Stop now. Stop. Don't need to go there this morning, do we. Been there. Done it far, far too many times. Wish you were here, brother dear, to gimme a hug. Some sugar May used to say.

Is it worse now. Doesn't seem possible, but it just might be. Not only for our family. Shit no. Not just us. Everybody. Everybody jammed up here wit us in this stinking mess. Everybody just too scared or too dumb to know it, is what our brother said with his eyes when I came to town to visit and we let go of each other and time for me to leave the prison and he has to stay where he is and nothing to do but look at each other one more time, one more sad, helpless stinking time. Clang, bang, gate shuts behind me and they still got the key.

We had talked about power during that visit. Talked in the cage. Power how long, too long stolen by the ruling group to diminish and control the ruled. Power of this political system that has operated from its start as if vast gaps dividing us from the ruling group either don't exist or don't matter. Same ole shit.

Ask the brothers in here, our brother says. Ask the outlaws. Ask them about law supposed to protect everybody—rulers and ruled—from each other equally. Law calling itself the will of the people. Law that got all us in here blackened up like minstrels. Color, His-Honor-Mr.-Law says, No problem. While out the other side of his mouth he's saying color gives law power to abuse color. Look at the color around us in here. Some days I look and cry. Laugh some days. Our colors, our group. Power serves itself. Period. Exclamation point. Truth and only truth, our locked-up brother says. And he's not wrong, our brother's not wrong, so how can I be right. My empire. They slam the gate shut. Blam. Time to leave my brother's cage, go back in mine. My maps. Ledgers. Theirs.

Remember when I called you couple weeks ago, Sis, and asked the man's name Daddy killed. Conversation got long, much longer than usual, nice in a way because usually conversations shortish because we skip over awful things and don't want to jinx good things by talking too much about them but I remember I think we both got deep into the begats, both trying to recall Daddy's grandmother's name and neither could and Owens popped into my mind and I said Owens to you and you said, Sybil Owens—wasn't she the slave from down south who came up here to found Homewood and you were right of course and I laughed because I was the one who wrote down the Sybela Owens story and you knew the story from my books or from family conversations. Same family conversations from which I'd learned, mostly from May, about May's grandmother or great-grandmother, Sybela, who had fled slavery with a white man who stole Sybela from his slave-plantation-owner father and settled in or near what's now called Homewood where one day when May was a little girl she saw, according to her, an old, old woman on a porch in a rocking chair smoking a pipe, woman in a long black dress, dark stockings, and head rag who smiled at her and she'd hear people say later the old woman was her grandmother, maybe great-grand, and May never forgot and passed on the memory or tale or whatever to us, a story about Mom's side of the family, not Daddy's, and I wrote or talked my version of it and you probably heard May herself tell it like I did but years and years ago and the best we usually do as we try to sort out the family tree and put names to branches, to people, is most likely to mix up things the way I did with *Owens* before you corrected my memory and I reminded myself and you how family stories were partly what one of us had heard live from the mouth of the one who had lived the story or heard it second- or thirdhand and passed it on but partly also stuff I had made up, written down, and it got passed around the family same as accounts of actual witnesses telling stories the way May told hers about Sybela so that day on the phone we were begatting this one from that one and so on, you said, Hold on a minute and went up to the attic where you keep those boxes and boxes of Mom's things, the papers and letters she saved from the old people in the family, because you believed there was an obituary in rough draft in Mom's hand on tablet paper that might tell us Daddy's grandmother's name, the name I could hear my father and Aunt C saying plain as day but could not raise beyond a whispering in my ear too faint to grasp or repeat aloud to myself. And sure enough you quickly retrieved information Mom had written down long ago for a church funeral program, maybe for the colored newspaper, too, a couple sheets of blue-lined school table paper, lines and handwriting faded, creases in the paper also cuts, the obituary notice we both had remembered but neither could repeat the exact contents of. You had the folded sheets in your hand in a minute once you got up those steep-assed attic steps I worry about my little sis climbing because she's not little sis anymore but sweet, still sweet.

Yes, you hear me talking to you, girl. This is eldest brother speaking, and you're my sweet sister and don't you dare sass me, girl. Two of our brothers gone, just us two left and our brother in the slam and when you read me Mom's notes for her father's obituary they included Daddy's name but do not mention our father's mother's mother so of course they solved nothing just deepened the puzzle of how and why and where and who we come from and here we are again, and whatever we discover about long ago, it never tells us enough, does it. Not what we are nor what comes next after all that mess we don't even know maybe or not happened before . . . well, we try . . . and after I listened to you reading bits of information the note compiled, I thought about the meaning of long ago, and how absolutely long ago separates past and present, about the immeasurable sadness, immeasurable distance that well up in me often when I hear the words *long ago,* and on another day, in another conversation, I will attempt to explain how certain words or phrases reveal more than I might choose to know, an unsettling awareness like seeing an ugly tail on an animal I know damn well has no tail or a tail negligible as the one people carry around and can't see, and I will ask you, Tish, what if I'm trying to imagine *long ago* and a shitty, terrible-looking tail appears, a tail like the one I'm sure doesn't belong on a familiar animal but grows longer, larger, and hides the animal. Wraps round and round and takes over. Will there be nothing left then, I will ask you. Nothing. Not even wishful thinking. The life, the long ago, once upon a time I am trying to imagine—gone like the animal not supposed to own a tail and the tail I inflicted upon it.

WRITING TEACHER

I hear from my former students occasionally. A few have gone on to accomplish remarkable work. Hear equally from the ordinary and remarkable. Requests for recommendations, announcements of new jobs, marriages, children, a photo, copy of a book or filmscript, story in a magazine or anthology, perhaps inscribed personally to me or sent directly from the publisher. The gift of a snapshot, book, or story meant to break silence that settles in after they leave the university, the silence that being here, a student for a semester in my fiction writing class, doesn't break, silence of living ordinary lives we all endure whether our writing is deemed remarkable by others or not.

A current student, Teresa McConnell, wants to help other people. The story she submits to my fiction writing class, though not very long, is quite ambitious. It wishes to save the life of its main character, a young woman of color, a few years out of high school, single, child to support, no money, shitty job, living with her mother who never misses an I-told-you-so chance to criticize her daughter's choices. Voice of the character my student invents to narrate the story reveals the young colored woman to be bright, articulate, thoughtful, painfully aware of how race, gender, age, poverty trap her. Worse now because a baby daughter is trapped with her. Lack of understanding not the narrator's problem. She's stifled by lack of resources, options.

What's a poor girl to do. My student's story, like the fictional young woman it portrays, begins and ends stuck in the midst of an apparently insoluble quandary. If the writer wants her fiction to aid actual people outside it, desires her words to be more than a well-intentioned display of good intentions, more than a dreary recital of a plight suffered by countless young, underprivileged women, the story requires help.

A desire to help is admirable, I think, and in order to help, I will set aside, for the moment, my doubts. Perform the job I'm paid for. Concentrate upon being supportive. Commend strong passages, point out inconsistencies, transparencies characteristic of an undergrad first draft, which, after all, the story is. Console Miss McConnell that every story—by a novice or Nobel laureate—begins life as a first draft.

I appreciate Miss McConnell's attempt to step outside herself, beyond this cloistered university world where the skin of an overwhelming majority of the students, including her skin, betrays no trace of colored people's color. My color, by the way. And lucky for her, not hers, since her father a bigot she will admit later, and he flat-out despises colored people. Her mother is different, she adds quietly. Mom taught me to respect people of all races, she says. And I don't ask Teresa McConnell, but I'm certainly curious which parent contributed more to her story's determination to help.

My student's story stuck like most people's because there's no place for it to go. Except to explore the sadness of wanting things not to be the way they indisputably are. A story begins with an author's desire to write it. Starts with a person the author happens to be.

Should I tell my student that in order to overcome the smothering inertia of helplessness, I'm currently reading biographies of Ludwig Wittgenstein and Catherine the Great, a novel, *A Dream in Polar Fog*, about Chukchi Eskimos, Joseph McElroy's stories in *Night Soul*. Contemplating retirement from my day job of college teaching. Resisting the possibility age might retire me from fiction writing. Coping with the likelihood that neither my imprisoned brother nor son will be released anytime soon. Negotiating with sexual desire, strong as ever, though it less reliably elicits a hard-on to fulfill it. Unlearning old-school verities of time, space, memory, identity while I shiver in the icy wind of the only certainty granted by a long, precipitously up-and-down life—its absolute extinction.

Of course hearing my story does not fix hers. Perhaps I should begin our conference by talking about a different story. Not mine, not hers. One less personal, though familiar to us both. For instance, Hans Christian Andersen's fairy tale about an emperor's invisible new clothes. Tell her I loved it the very first time I read it or it was read to me, a colored boy hungry for books, for stories that rescued him from the dismal poverty and unpromising futures of his life. Confess to her my instant envy of the bold kid who exposes a naked emperor. Explain how Andersen's seductively simple fable has grown more complicated as I've aged. Its subject not a guileless, helplessly honest boy, not the foibles of a particular pitiful guy who happens to be emperor, but *empire*. Empire's power to enthrall, lobotomize, oppress. To ensnare us within our own fantasies. Our vanity, willed innocence, terror.

How can I teach Ms. McConnell that it is impossible to write a story without a naked little wannabe emperor squirreled away inside. Let's undress your story, Ms. McConnell, I could say. Except that invitation too suggestive for a teacher to propose to a student. Even though it would be easier to school her if she, I, the story naked.

Instead I play it safer. We keep on our clothes. Stick close to the text. In its very first sentence, with its fifth word, Miss McConnell, your story addresses a "you." The character who is your narrator warns that "you," reader, would be pummeled by tiny fists if her daughter burst suddenly from the phone booth of her crib, masked, caped, armed with the superpowers all down-and-out, unwed, teen mothers daydream for their kids. To avoid this beating, reader, "you" better listen up. Change your ways. Surrender privileges that victimize others and drive them to strike back with baby punches or terrorist bombs.

I advise my students that identifying readers as the enemy too early in a story not the wisest strategy. Nobody likes being called out. Pronounced guilty without a trial. Readers bad-mouthed are same readers the story endeavors to woo. The "you" in Teresa McConnell's first sentence too inclusive. Casts a net wide enough to catch her racist dad, her tolerant mom, me, you, people who sneer at reading fiction, curious people who love to read stories. No story able to help everybody. No story is smarter than all its readers.

Lighten up, I remind myself. Don't sound like the narrator's carping mother. Attempts to be playful a virtue of Miss McConnell's draft. Why shouldn't her story, like this story, pose a few teasing, little, unthreatening threats.

In spite of my intention not to infringe upon any students' writerly prerogatives, I feel obliged to remind them that making up a story also entails making up both an author and an audience. Word by word a story welcomes some readers, shoos others away. Paints faces on invisible characters outside it as well as inside. A face for the author hovering precariously both inside and out. Author who swoops around at warp speed in galaxies no one else has ever seen.

We, my student and I, not characters in a sci-fi drama located in hyperspace. We are seated at a small, round table inside an office outside the story. An office set aside for me a few hours a week inside a university building. Outside the brick building a large city spreads, and if this borrowed university cubicle owned a window, we could see whether snow still falls outside as it was falling earlier this morning on a city that starts or ends at a wall of concrete, steel, and glass towers lining the sea. Inside this city is a house my student resides in with her family, not rich not poor, not a colored family, so she's not a colored daughter falling between society's cracks, unwed, broke, child to raise, stuck in a dead-end job, bills, bills, more bills, and more trashy jobs to pay them until the end of time. No, that's definitely not her, according to the backstory Teresa McConnell recites as she speaks briefly about herself. My curiosity, no matter how professorially, how gently I probe, would be invasive of her privacy, so I don't pursue more than the little she volunteers. Story she's written for my class enough. Should reveal all the author wishes readers, including me, to know about her.

We're not characters inside the story we sit and discuss inside this office. We only pretend we are. No one's life is at stake. Words on the page are the reason we are meeting. My student's words are what they are. Words. They contain the story, although you could just as appropriately suggest the story contains them. You could say the text is what I desire to help or say that the fact she's written a text intended to help other people is why I want to help her. None of the above helps much, you might be thinking. World remains as it is—resistant, opaque, you may also be thinking, and is the "you" I'm imagining the same presumptive "you" her story calls out in its initial sentence.

One thing for certain I can say: my student's not the young brown woman inside the story. No one in the universe is that young colored woman. However, in one game a story can play she exists. In another game she doesn't. In another game no game exists, only you and I exist, and not for sure, not for long.

Which game are you playing, I could ask Teresa McConnell. Are readers supposed to pretend you exist or don't exist inside your story. Both. Neither. Are good writers able to help readers negotiate such issues. Does compassion trump technique or technique trump compassion. Is it okay to borrow another's identity in order to perpetrate a good deed. If you don't obtain the other's permission, are you an identity thief.

Isn't your story, like every story, a masquerade, Miss McConnell. Why do you believe your disguise is working. Do you care if your mask slips and uncovers your face. I often worry mine's slipping.

So let's look closer. Together, Teresa. I believe we both care. Look right here, page 3, where your young woman's infuriated by a smug, smart-ass emergency-room clerk who assumes that the female in front of him, because she is young and colored, won't own health insurance to pay a doctor to sew up a bloody gash in her daughter's head. Why not have your young woman kill him and turn your story into that story.

Show not tell. Don't bother telling me or telling a young woman you are on her side and wish to help. She doesn't need that kind of help. She's quite as capable as you are of dealing with an obnoxious clerk. Your story depicts her as stuck much deeper. She needs more than words, your story says. So maybe chopping off the clerk's head a way out. A way out of the story and out of yourself, too. Risk letting her do what you would never do. Then maybe the young woman will speak for herself, not you. Speak with action not words. Break free, break bad outside the story's boundaries.

Nobody wrote John Brown's story before he committed the acts that created his story. Nobody could pretend to be him or speak for him or hate or love him until John Brown smote his enemies in Kansas and perpetrated a bloody raid on Harpers Ferry to free slaves. No John Brown story, no John Brown, no Civil War until he showed the way. His way. His acts. The war inside him exploding outside.

Who believes they can experience what another person experiences. Wouldn't a person be many people if such an exchange possible.

I wish I were in love with my student. Maybe it would be easier. Maybe for thirty minutes in this office, maybe during the moments I desire to help her, I am. I do. And help myself. The pair of us celebrating the end of empire. Empire that traps us and neither of us loves. Of course we don't. We wait for it to tip over, fall down, and go boom. A vast reverberating, silent crash changing everything. Us, this office, university, city outside, nation inside which the city resides, nation inside the idea of empire wrapped so carefully strand by strand, silk and steel cable of spider webbing wrapped round and round endlessly, a transparent cocoon holding everything inside, binding everything together until in one quiet, crystal-clear instant we decide to say—No. Nothing's there. Emperor naked. Empire naked.

We wait and wait for the moment to arrive. Wait for the time to celebrate. Time to love. We understand empire a chimera, a bad idea. Same bad idea over and over again. Empire dead. Long live empire.

Dark, dark, darker when empire failing. We chew on nothing and nothing lasts a long, long time. We dream and starve and die. We wait. Hope to survive as subjects of the next empire.

So here we sit, my student, Teresa McConnell, and I, awaiting our liberation, our chance to help one another. To celebrate. In this office, this moment. Though around us, inside us, something keeps us in place. A story more powerful, more hungry, more implacable than any one of ours will ever be.

Anyway, the story on the table not mine, I say. It's absolutely yours, I reassure my student, and you must always feel free, feel more than welcome, Teresa, to discard my advice, anybody's advice.

She smiles. I think she's beginning to relax in spite of the uncomfortable surroundings, this unnatural exchange. I believe she senses my desire to help. Perhaps she's offering me what she expects for her story, for herself. No more, no less than the benefit of the doubt. I repeat to her that I truly have no desire nor interest in seeing her change what she's written so it conforms to my ideas. Difficult enough, impossible enough, I say, to revise my own stuff.

She nods and smiles again. On the table her story lies open to the third page, where a young admissions clerk insults a young, brown-skinned mother.

Tomorrow, I want to confide to Teresa. Tomorrow, Teresa, I will gaze up from words on the page and our eyes will meet. Tomorrow, I will tell her that I'm going to look into the possibility of obtaining a weapon. Haven't decided yet the best way to deploy it, if and when I get one. Whatever kind of weapon it turns out to be. Arming myself is the first step. Figuring out the next step the harder part—scale, location, how to maximize what might very well be my single chance to help, chance to inflict damage on the empire. Assassinate a sadistic prison guard, chairperson of a corrupt, merciless pardons and parole board. Blow up a building, an airplane, take hostages. Write a story. Fall in love. Raid Harpers Ferry.

Your asshole clerk, I will say. Deal with him. Your way, Teresa. Marry him. Murder him. Whatever. Your way, I will reiterate. Then I must be careful to add, Please ignore my crazy digressions, my playful revisions. They are not as innocent as the baby fists in your story.

Inside my head I see empires of my desire, empires of my revenge topple and kick up clouds of dust around my feet as they bury themselves, words spoken and unspoken. I suppress my dream of power, a fantasy I might possess an idea to improve myself or society, let alone possess the means to show any single person what she should or shouldn't do next. I revise. Lean closer to my student for emphasis.

Your clerk, Teresa. This is the point or rather he's the point where for me the energies within your story converge, crackle, glow. He's about your age, your social and economic class more or less, your color more or less, a color, wisely or not, unspecified by your story but hardly irrelevant, I'd guess, since you imply his color inspires his ugly reaction to the young colored woman.

I think or rather my opinion or rather what I feel is that the clerk is you, Teresa. Something about you, about your father, your mother, me. We're all inside that young guy and he's inside us and that's what allows him to be able and willing to marshal hundreds of years of history, of pillage, blood, suffering, and squash someone or maybe not try to squash, maybe just contain, maybe just loosen a little or sometimes just squeeze the wraps slightly tighter to test, to practice controlling them. Exercising them to make sure they are in place. To be certain they include, surround, protect us. Like the bonds of a story that hold it together and make sense of everything. Of a moment in which the clerk finds his job compels him to serve a young colored female who by God should expect nothing from him, who on the contrary should be serving him or grateful to him for whatever service she receives, who should make it apparent to him, always with humility and deference, that she's well aware that the invisible strands permitting her to believe she has a right to ask him for help also license him, as he performs his numbing job, to despise her, abuse her, despise himself as he pretends to help so empire won't crash down on both their heads.

Deal with him, with that, Teresa. As I must deal with my responsibilities. Teacher and elder. Subject of empire. Inventor of fictions.

Should I also share with my student an unsettling image that intrudes these days when I attempt to situate myself within this nation we inhabit. How I see young people returning from war. Daily, coast to coast, they are landing here and there in small airports and large, in bus depots, unpatrolled spots along interstates, smell of war still in their clothes, in their nostrils, blood dark on hands they furiously, secretly, silently scrub and scrub like Lady Macbeth, wasn't it, I think. Think maybe I'll teach *Macbeth* next semester or something from Shakespeare, anyway. *Tempest*, perhaps, or Melville's *Benito Cereno* or narratives from Chernobyl a

Russian woman recorded or Ellison's *Invisible Man* because what else to say to them, how to help.

A few of these young people may receive a government bounty for school and a few of that few might migrate to a class like yours, Teresa, this class in which you seek help to write a story. A story to help others, story for a class in which my job is to help. The prospect terrifies me.

Whether or not any survivors of war wind up in my creative writing classroom, where are the rest. The ones I think of as veterans returning, and the ones killed in action, and the appalling number who die here inside our country each week by their own hands.

How many alive only an instant in these killing fields before they are gone forever. How many does it take to disturb the frozen quiet, black glisten of empire. To penetrate, agitate, produce movement. Not the empire's dead invisible carcass thrashing darkly. Something else moving I try to detect in your eyes. In your story.

Where do they go. The ones coming back from combat, jails, exile, from being forgotten, tortured, ignored, from being buried alive. Not spoken of. Spoken for. Your young colored woman, her baby, that kid working at the hospital desk. You. Me.

I poke out a hand to break silence as we both rise. We shake shyly. Our chairs groan chair noise. See you next week, Teresa.

WILLIAMSBURG BRIDGE

Quick trip yesterday so today I'm certain and determined to jump, though not in any hurry. Why should I be. All the time in the world at my disposal. All of it. Every invisible iota. No beginning. No end. Whole load. Whole wad. All mine the moment I let go. Serene, copious, seamless time.

How much of it do you believe you possess. Enough of it to spare a stranger the chump change of a moment or two while he sits on Williamsburg Bridge, beyond fences that patrol the pedestrian walkway, on a forbidden edge where a long steel rail or pipe runs parallel to walkways, bikeways, highways, and train tracks supported by this enormous towering steel structure that supports us, too, sky above, East River below, this edge where the bridge starts and terminates in empty air.

To be absolutely certain, I rode the F train yesterday from my relatively quiet Lower East Side neighborhood to Thirty-Fourth Street and set myself adrift in crowds always flailing around Penn Station and Herald Square. To be certain of what. Certain I had no desire to repeat the experience. Certain that experience consists of repetition and that what repeats is the certainty of nothing new. Short subway ride uptown in dark tunnels beneath New York's sidewalks, twenty-five, thirty minutes of daylight aboveground, among countless bodies shrieking, shuddering, hurtling ahead like trains underground, each one on its single, blind track and I was certain once more of the sad, frightening thoroughness of damage people inflict upon themselves and others, of a fallen city embracing us, showcasing the results of a future beyond repair. Certain I was prepared to sit here a short while and then let go.

I believe I heard Sonny Rollins playing his sax on Williamsburg Bridge one afternoon so many years ago I can't recall the walkway's color back then. Old color was definitely not what it is now: pale reds and mottled pinks of my tongue as I wag it at myself each morning in the mirror. Iron fences with flaking paint that's cotton-candy pink frame the entrance to the bridge at the intersection of Delancey and Clinton Streets where I stepped onto it today for the very last time, passing through monumental stone portals, then under a framework of steel girders that span the bridge's 118-foot width and display steel letters announcing its name.

Just beyond shoulder-high, rust-acned rails, a much taller crimson barrier of heavy-gauge steel chicken wire bolted to sturdy steel posts guards the fences. Steel crossbeams, spaced four yards or so apart, form a kind of serial roof over the walkway, too high by about a foot for me to jump up and touch, even on my best days playing hoop. Faded red crossties overhead could be rungs of a giant ladder that once upon a time had slanted up into the sky but now lies flat, rungs separated by gaps of sky that seem to open wider as I walk beneath them, though if I lower my eyes and gaze ahead into the distance where the bridge's far end should be, the walkway's a tunnel, solid walls and ceiling converge, no gaps, no exit, a mauvish gray cul-de-sac.

Tenor sax wail is the color I remember from the afternoon decades ago I heard Sonny Rollins the first and only time live. Color deeper than midnight blue. Dark, scathing, grudging color of a colored soldier's wound coloring dirty white bandages wrapped around his dark chest. An almost total eclipse of color while dark blood slowly drip drop drip drops from mummy wrap into the snow. A soldier bleeding, an unknown someone testifying on a sax and the chance either one will survive the battlefield highly unlikely.

I don't want to weigh down my recollection with too much gloomy symbolism so let's just say it was a clear afternoon a sax turned blacker than night. Color of all time. Vanished time. No time. Dark smudge like I mix from ovals of pure, perfect color in the paint box I found under the Christmas tree one morning when I was a kid. Unexpected color with a will of its own brewed by a horn's laments, amens, witness. That's what I remember, anyway. Color of disappointment, of ancient injuries and bruises and staying alive and dying and being born again all at once after I had completed about half the first lap of a back-and-forth hump over the Williamsburg Bridge.

Walking the bridge is an old habit now. One I share with numerous other walkers whose eyes avoid mine as I avoid theirs, our minds perhaps on people down below, people alive and dead on tennis courts, ball fields, running tracks, swings, slides, benches, chairs, blankets, grass plots, gray paths alongside the East River.

Not exactly breaking news, is it, that from up here human beings seem tiny as ants. Too early this morning for most people or ants, but from this height, this perch beyond walkway fences, this railing or pipe along an out-of-bounds edge of Williamsburg Bridge, I see a few large ants or little people sprinkled here and there. Me way up here, ants and people way down there all the same size. Same weight. Same fate. Same crawl. Inching along inside the armor of our solitary-nesses. Hi-ho. Hi-Ho. Off to work we go.

So here I am, determined to jump, telling myself, telling you that I'm certain. Then what's the fool waiting for, it's fair for you to ask. My answer: *certain* an old-fashioned word in a world where, at best, I'm able only to approximate the color of a bridge I've walked across thousands of times, a world where the smartest people acknowledge an uncertainty principle and run things accordingly and own just about everything and make fools of the vast majority of the rest of us not as smart, not willing to endure lives without certain certainties. In this world where desire for certainty is a cage most people lock themselves in and throw away the key, I don't wish to be a victim, a complete dupe, so I hedge my bets. I understand certainty is always relative, and not a very kind, generous, loving relative I can trust, especially since the uncertainty principle enfolds everybody equally, smart or dumb, no matter. Which is to say, or rather to admit, that although I'm sure I'm up here and sure this edge is where I wish to be and sure of what I intend to do next, I can't be truly certain, only as close to certain as you or I will ever get, before the instant I let go.

Many years passed before I figured out it had to be Sonny Rollins I had heard. Do you know who I mean. Theodore Walter

Rollins, born September 7, 1930, New York City—emerges early fifties, "most brash innovative creative young tenor player"—flees to Chicago to escape perils of NYC jazz scene—reemerges 1955 in NYC with Clifford Brown, Max Roach group—nicknamed Newk for resemblance to Don Newcombe, star Brooklyn Dodgers pitcher—produces string of great albums before he withdraws from public again—practices on the Williamsburg Bridge "to get self together after too much fame, too soon"—returns with new album, *The Bridge*—another sabbatical, Japan, India, "to get himself together" . . . thinks, "it's a good thing for anybody to do" . . . etc. etc.—all this information available at Sonny Rollins website—although cocaine addiction, a year he did at Rikers for armed robbery are not in his website bio.

Once I'd become sure I had heard Sonny Rollins playing live, my interest, my passion for his music escalated. As did my intimacy with the Williamsburg Bridge. Recently, trying to discover where it ranks among New York bridges in terms of its attractiveness to jumpers, I came across AlexReisner.com/NYC2 and a story about a suicide in progress on the Williamsburg Bridge that Mr. Reisner claimed to witness. Numerous black-and-white photos illustrate his piece. In some pictures a young colored man wears neatly cropped dreads, pale skin, pale undershorts, a bemused expression, light mustache, shadow of beard, his hands curled around a pipe/rail running along the outermost edge of the bridge where he sits. Water ripples behind, below to frame him. His gaze downcast, engaged elsewhere, a place no one else on the planet can see. No people there, no time there where his eyes have drifted, settled. His features regular, handsome in a stiff, plain, old-fashioned way. Some mother's mixed son, mixed-up son.

If I could twist around, shift my weight without losing balance, rotate my head pretty drastically for a chronically stiff neck and glance over my left shoulder, I'd see what the pale young man probably saw, the superimposed silhouettes of the Manhattan and the Brooklyn Bridges downriver, grand cascades of steel cables draped from their towers, and over there if I stay steady and focused, I could pick out the tip of the Statue of Liberty jutting just above Brooklyn Bridge, Miss Liberty posed like sprinters Tommie Smith and John Carlos on the winners' stand at the 1968 Mexico City Olympics, her torch a black-gloved fist rammed into the sky: Up yours. We're number one. Stadium in an uproar, Go boys go. I see a fuming Hitler grab his cockaded, tricornered hat and split like he did in '36. In the haze where sky meets sea and both dissolve, a forest of tall cranes and derricks, arms canted at the exact angle of the Statue's arm, return her victory salute.

Dawns on me that I'll miss the next Olympics, next March Madness, next Super Bowl. Dawns on me that I won't regret missing them. A blessing. Free at last. Dawns on me I won't miss missing them any more than all the sports I won't be watching on TV will miss me.

If I still have your attention, I suppose I should say more about why I'm here, prepared to jump. It's not because I won or didn't win a gold medal. Not up here to sell shoes or politics. Nor because my mom's French. Not here because of my color or lack of color. My coloring pale like the young colored man in website photos who sat, I believe, precisely on the spot where I'm sitting. Color not the reason I'm here nor the reason you are here, whatever you call your color. Mine, it appears, gives an impression of palish sepia or beige. The sprinters' black fists, taut arms holler forget about it. Forget the yes or no, misfortune or fortune, lack or surplus of pigment your skin displays. Ain't about color. Speed what it's about. Color just a gleam in the beholder's eye. Now you see it, now you don't.

On the other hand, no doubt, color matters. My brownish tinge, gift of the colored man my mother married, confers added protection against sunburn in tropical climates and a higher degree of social acceptance generally in some nations or regions or communities within nations or regions where people more or less my color are the dominant majority. My color also produces in many people of other colors an adverse reaction as hardwired as a worker ant's love for the nest's queen. Thus color keeps me on my toes. Danger and treachery never far removed from any person's life regardless of color, but in my case, danger and treachery are palpable, everyday presences. No surprise at all. Unpleasantness life inflicts, no matter how terrible, also glimmers with confirmation. Told you so, Color smiles.

Gender not the reason I'm here either. A crying shame in this advanced day and age that plenty of people would tag my posture as effeminate. See a little girlish girl on a couch squeezing her thighs together because she's too shy in company to get up and go pee. A suspicious posture for a male, especially a guy with pale cheeks and chin noticeably shadowed by stubble. Truth is with my upper body tilted slightly backward, weight poised on my rear end, arms thrust out to either side for balance, hands like the young man's in the photo gripping a fat pipe or rail, I must press my thighs together to maintain stability. Keep my feet spread apart so they serve as bobbing anchors.

Try it sometime. Someplace high and dangerous, ideally. You'll get the point. Point being of course any position you assume up here unsafe. Like choice of a language, gender, color, etc. People forced to choose, forced to suffer the consequences. No default settings. Like choosing which clothes to wear on the Williamsburg Bridge or not wear. I've chosen to keep my undershorts on. I want to be remembered as a swimmer not some naked nut. Swimmer who has decided to swim away, dignity intact. Homely but perfectly respectable boxers serving as proxies for swimming trunks. Just about naked also because I don't wish to be mistaken for a terrorist. No intent to harm a living soul. Or dead souls. No traffic accidents, boat accidents caused by my falling body, heavier and heavier, they say, as it descends. No concealed weapons, no dynamite strapped around my bare belly. No excuse for cops to waste me unless they're scared of what's inside my shorts, and I sympathize with their suspicions. Understand cops are pledged to protect us, guarantee our security. We live in troubled times. Who doubts it. Who can tell what's in the mind of a person sitting next to you on a subway or standing at the adjacent public urinal. Anyway, either way, gunned down or not, I've taken pains to situate myself on the bridge's outermost edge to maximize the chance I hit nothing but water, no collateral damage.

And contrary to what you might be thinking, loneliness has not driven me to the edge. I'm far from lonely. With all the starving, homeless people on the planet, don't waste any pity on me, please. In addition to my undershorts I have pain, grief, plenty of regrets, dismal expectations of the future to keep me company, and when not entertained sufficiently by those companions I look down below. Whole shitty world's at my feet.

My chilly toes wiggle like antennae, my chilly thighs squeeze together not because of loneliness. They move with purpose like my mother's hands forming a steeple. You might think she's about to pray, but then she chants: *Here's the church/See the steeple,* words that start a game Mom taught me in ancient days. Hand jive. I can't stop a grin spreading across my face even here, today, when she begins rhyming and steeples her pale, elegant fingers. I'm a sucker every time. *Here's the church/See the steeple.* I close my eyes—cathedrals, towers, castles, cities materialize in thin air—la-di-da . . . la-di-da. I drift entranced till she cries: *Open the doors/Out come the people.* Then her fingertips hordes of tiny wiggly people who poke, tickle, grab, nibble, pinch. I giggle, and she laughs out loud. I double over to protect my softest, most ticklish spots. Her nails dig into my ribs, fingers chase me up under my clothes. My small body squirms, thrashes every which way on her lap. No escape. Stoppit. Stoppit. Please, Mom. Stop or I'll fall. Please don't stop.

Yes, Mom. One could say I drink a lot, Mom, and drink perhaps part of the problem, but not why I'm up here. Do I drink too much—yes/no—lots of wine—it's usually wine—often good French wine and even so, yes, too much disturbs my customary way of coolly processing things and making sense of what I observe. Drink a bad habit, I admit. Like hiring a blind person to point out what my eyes miss. But I'm grateful to the potbellied wine god. Drink simpatico, an old, old cut-buddy. I gape at his antics, the damage he causes, stunned by the ordinary when it shows itself through his eyes. The ordinary. Only that, Mom. Nothing evil, nothing extreme, nothing more or less than the ordinary showing itself as gift, a wolf in sheep's clothing. Then naked. The ordinary exposed when I'm drinking. You must know what I mean. I'm the hunter who wants to shoot it. Wants to be eaten.

French my dead mother's mother tongue and occasionally I think in French. Mother tongue swabs my gums, wraps around my English, swallows it. Gears of the time machine whir in sync with French—ooh-la-la. I nearly swoon. Mother's tongue, French words in my mouth. Thinking in French. French the only language in the universe.

If another person appeared next to me sitting on the steel rail where I sit and the person asked—What do you mean by "mother tongue"—what do you mean, "think in French"—I would have to answer: "I don't know." Carefully speak the words aloud in English, those exact words repeated twice to keep track of language, of where I am, to keep track of myself.

Truth is, "I don't know." I falter, no more truth follows. Too late. Time machine whirs on, leaves nothing behind, nothing ahead, no words I'm able to say to steady myself after I scramble to make room for another on the rail. Desperate to explain before we tumble off the edge. Desperate to translate a language one and only one person in the universe speaks, has ever spoken. I struggle to open a parenthesis and hold it open, keep a space uncluttered, serene, safe. Me inside it able to gather my thoughts, my words before they disintegrate, before the machine whirs on, before its spinning gears crush, consume, before the temple walls collapse, rubble around my feet, rats darting through the ruins from corpse to bloated corpse for the sweetest bits, blood squishing between my toes. Words silenced, rushing away, tongue dead meat in my mouth.

What words will I be saying to myself the instant I slip or pitch backward into the abyss. Will French words or Chinese or Yoruba make a difference. Will I return from the East River with a new language in my head, start up the universe again with new words, or do I leave it all behind, everything behind forever, the way thoughts leave me behind. Thoughts which smash like eggs on the unforgiving labyrinth's walls. Can I scrape off dripping goo. Twist it into a string to lead me out of whitespace.

East River behind me, below me, is not whitespace. River showing off today. Chilly ripples scintillate under cold, intermittent sunshine. If someone snapped pictures of me, like the ones Reisner snapped of a young colored man, several photos would show water darkly framing my pale flesh, in others my skin darker than water. Water colors differently depending on point of view, light, wind, cosmic dissonance. Water shows all colors, no color, any color from impenetrable oily sludge to purest glimmer. Water a medium like whitespace yet drastically unlike whitespace. From water springs mother, father, posterity, progress, all vitality, even so-called insensible matter. Whitespace empty. Above, below, before, after, always. Whitespace thin, thin ice. Blank pages words skate across before they vanish. Whitespace disguises itself as spray, as froth, as bubbles, as a big, white splash when I let go and land in the East River. My ass-backwards swan dive, swan song greeted by white applause, a bouquet of white flames while deep down below, whitespace swallows, burps, closes blacker than night.

But no. Not yet. I'm in no hurry this morning. Not afraid either. Fear not the reason I'm up here, ready to jump. I may be clutching white-knuckled onto the very edge of a very high bridge, but I don't fear death, don't feel close to death. I've felt more fear of death, much closer to death on numerous occasions. Closest one summer evening under streetlights in the park in the ghetto where I used to hoop. Raggedy outdoor court, a run available every evening except on summer weekends when the high-flyers owned it. A daily pickup game for older gypsies like me wandering in from various sections of the city, for youngblood wannabes from the neighborhood, local has-beens and never-wases, a run perfect for my mediocre, diminishing skills, high-octane fantasies, an aging body that enjoyed pretending to be in superb condition, at least for the first five or six humps up and down the Cyclone-fenced court, getting off with the other players as if it's the NBA finals, our chance at last to show we're contenders. Ferocious play war, harmless fun unless you get too enthusiastic, one too many flashbacks to glory days which never existed and put a move on somebody that puts you out of action a couple weeks, couple months, for good if you aren't careful. Anyway, one evening a hopped-up gangster and his crew cruise up to the court in a black, glistening Lincoln SUV. Bogart winners and our five well on the way to delivering the righteous ass-kicking the chumps deserved for stealing a game from decent folks waiting in line for a turn. Mr. Bigtime, bigmouth, big butt dribbles the ball off his foot, out of bounds. Calls foul. Then boots the pill to the fence. Waddle-waddling after it, he catches up and plants a foot atop it. Tired of this punk-ass, jive-ass run, he announces. Motherfucker over, motherfuckers. Then he unzips the kangaroo pouch of a blimpy sweat top he probably never sheds no matter how hot on the court because it hides a tub of jelly-belly ba-dup, ba-dupping beneath it, and from the satiny pullover extracts a very large pistol. Steps back, nudges the ball forward with his toe and—Pow—kills the poor thing as it tries to roll away. Pow—Pow—Pow—starts to shooting up the court. Everybody running, ducking to get out the goddamned fool's way. Gwan home, niggers. Ain't no more got-damn game today. Pow. King of the court, ruler of the hood, master of the universe. Pow. Busy as he is during his rampage brother finds time to wave his rod in my direction. What you looking at, you yellow-ass albino motherfucker. Gun steady an instant, pointed directly between my eyes long enough I'm certain he's going to blow me away and I just about wet myself. If truth be told, with that cannon in my mug, maybe I did leak a little. In the poor light of the playground who could tell. Who cares is what I was thinking if I was thinking anything at that moment besides dead. Who knows. Who cares. Certainly not me, not posterity, not the worker ants wearing rubber aprons and rubber gloves who dump my body on a slab at the morgue, drag off my sneakers, snip off my hoop shorts and undershorts with huge shears before they hose me down. Sweat or piss or shit or blood in my drawers. Who knows. Who cares.

A near-death experience I survived to write a story about, a story my mother read and wrote a note about in one of the pamphlets from church she saved in neat stacks on top and under the night table beside her bed, pamphlets containing Bible verses and commentary to put herself to sleep.

I saw the note only after Mom died. A message evidently intended for my benefit she never got around to showing me. She had underlined words from Habakkuk that the pamphlet deemed appropriate for the first Sunday after Pentecost—"destruction and violence are before me; strife and contention arise. So the law becomes slack and justice never prevails—their own might is their god"—and in the pamphlet's margin she had printed a response to my story.

Of course I had proudly presented a copy of the anthology containing my story to my mother, one of two complimentary copies, by the way, all I ever received from the publisher as payment. Mom thanked me profusely, close to tears, I believe I recall, the day I placed the book in her hands, but afterwards she never once mentioned my story. I found her note by chance years later when I was sorting through boxes full of her stuff, most of it long overdue to be tossed. Pamphlet in my hand and suddenly Mom appears. Immediately after reading her note, I rushed off to read all of Habakkuk in the beat-up, rubber-band-bound Bible she had passed on to me, the Bible once belonging to my father's family, only thing of his she kept when he walked out of our lives, she said and said he probably forgot it, left it behind in his rush to leave. I searched old journals of mine for entries recorded around the date of the pamphlet, date of my story's publication. After this flurry of activity, I just about wept. My mother a busy scribbler herself, surprise, surprise, I had discovered, but a no-show as far as ever talking about her writing or mine. Then a message after she's gone, ghost message Mom doesn't show me till she's a ghost, too: This reminds me of your story about playing ball.

Why hadn't she spoken to me. Did she understand, after all, my great fear and loneliness. How close I've always felt to death. Death up in my face on the playground in the park. Nobody, nothing, no time between me and the end. Probably as near to death that moment as any living person gets. Closest I've ever felt to dying, that's for damn sure. Still is. So absolutely close and not even close at all, it turns out, cause here I sit.

Yo. All youall down below. Don't waste your breath feeling sorry for me. Your behinds may hit the water before mine.

With my fancy new phone I once googled the number of suicides each day in America. I'm a latecomer to the Internet, cell phones, iPads, all the incredible devices invented to connect people. Remain astounded by what must be for most younger folk commonplace transactions. By speaking a few words into my phone I learned 475 suicides per year, 1.3 daily in New York City. With a few more words or clicks one could learn yearly rates of suicide in most countries of the civilized world. Data more difficult obviously to access from prehistory, the bad old days before a reliable someone started counting everything, keeping score of everything, but even ancient numbers available, I discover, if you ask a phone the correct questions in the proper order. Answers supplied by sophisticated algorithms that estimate within a hairbreadth, no doubt, unknown numbers from the past. Lots of statistics re suicide, but I could not locate the date of the very first suicide nor find a chat room or blog offering lively debate on the who, when, why, where of the original suicide. You'd think someone would care about such a transformative achievement or at least an expert would claim credit for unearthing the first suicide's name and address, posting it for posterity.

Suicide of course a morbid subject. Who would want to know too much about it. Let's drop it. I'm much more curious about immortality and rapture, aren't you. Houston airport my prime candidate for a site where immortality might be practiced. First time I wandered round and round, part of a vast crowd shuffling through the maze of Houston airport's endless corridors and gates, my unoriginal reaction was: I did not know death had undone so many. But since I'm not morbid, I revised my thinking—perhaps these countless souls, these faces morphing into every face I've ever seen or remembered or forgotten, folks I had yet to meet or never would, faces from dreams, very specific avatars of flesh-and-blood faces (John Wayne's for instance) from books, magazines, TV, films, faces from the Rolodex of my imaginary lives, perhaps all these travelers not the dead. Maybe they are an ever-changing panorama of all people ever born and still to be born roaming through Houston airport. Immortality one colossal, permanent game of musical chairs. If one chair pulled out from under you, keep on trucking. Another empty chair to plop down on soon as that stranger or old buddy moves his or her fat ass. Just be patient, keep shuffling along, we're all old friends here, the whole gang's here. No planes arrive, no planes leave anybody's got to catch. Just keep strolling, smiling. Plenty of refreshments, souvenirs to buy. TV monitors and restrooms handy everywhere. The possibility of romance or peace and quiet or maybe even rapture, who knows what you'll find. Immortality a single life, a single airport waiting area we all share materializing as ourselves and others, moving round and round, swimming in an ocean, a drop of ourselves, same water, same airport no one leaves no one enters but everybody winds up there. Like you wind up a clock to tell time, to see time. Hear it and pretend time exists because the clock tick-tocks and whirs on—ba-dup, ba-dup.

If a person intent on suicide also seeking rapture, why not choose the Williamsburg Bridge. Like the young man in the website photos who probably believed his fall, his rapture would commence immersed within the colors of Sonny Rollins's tenor sax. Sonny's music first and last thing heard as water splashes open and seals itself—ba-dup. Rapture rising, a pinpoint spark of immortal dazzle ascending the heavens, wake spreading behind it, an invisible band of light that expands slowly, surely as milky-white wakes of water taxis passing beneath the bridge expand and shiver to the ends of the universe.

Sometimes it feels like I've been sitting up here forever. An old, weary ear worn out by nagging voices nattering inside and outside it. Other times I feel brand new, as if I've just arrived or not quite here yet, never will be. Lots to read here, plenty of threats, promises, advice, prophecies in various colors, multiple scripts scrawled, scrolled, stenciled, sprayed on the walkway's blackboard of pavement—*We will be Ephemeral—Mene Mene Tekel—Ends Coming Soon.* I've read elsewhere that boys in Asia Minor duel with kites of iridescent rainbow colors, a razor fixed to each kite's string to decide who's king, decide how long.

Clearly my kite's been noticed. Don't you see them. Bridge crawling with creepy, crawly cops in jumpsuits, a few orange, most the color of roaches. Swarms of them sneaky fast and brutal as always. They clamber over barriers, scuttle across girders, shimmy up cables, skulk behind buttresses, swing on ropes like Spider-Man. A chopper circles—Whomp-Whomp-Whomp-Whomp. One cop hoots through a bullhorn or karaoke mic. Will they shoot me off the bridge like they blasted poor, lovesick King Kong off the Empire State Building. Cop vehicles, barricades, flashing lights clog arteries that serve the bridge and its network of expressways, throughways, serviceways, overpasses, and underpasses, which should be pumping traffic noise and carbon monoxide to keep me company up here.

With a cell phone, if I could manage to dial it without dumping my ass in the frigid East River, I could call 911, leave a number for SWAT teams in the field to reach me up here, an opportunity for opposing parties to conduct a civilized conversation this morning instead of screaming back and forth like fishwives. My throat hoarse already, eyes tearing in the wicked wind. I will threaten to let go and plunge into the water if they encroach one inch further into my territory, my show this morning. On my way elsewhere and nobody's business if I do, chirps my friend, Ladyday.

Small clusters of ant people, people ants peer up at me now. What do they think they see tottering on the edge of Williamsburg Bridge. They appear to stare intently, concerned, curious, amused, though I've read numerous species of ant and certain specialists within numerous ant species nearly blind. Nature not wasting eyes on lives spent entirely in the dark. But nature generous, too, provides ants with antennae as proxies for vision and we get cell phones to cope with the blues.

Shared cell phone blues once with a girlfriend I had high hopes for once who told me about a lover once, her Michelangelo, gorgeous she said, a rod on him hard as God's wrath is how she put it, a pimp who couldn't understand why she got so upset when he conducted business by cell phone while lying naked next to naked her, a goddamn parade of women coming and going in my bedroom and Michelangelo chattering away as if I don't exist, him without a clue he was driving me crazy jealous she said and her with no clue how crazy jealous it was driving me, the lethal combination of my unhealthy curiosity and her innocent willingness to regale me with details of her former intimacies, her chattering away on her end and me listening on mine, connected and unconnected, cell phone blues until listening just about killed me and I had to let her go and lost her like she lost her sweet Michelangelo.

Not expecting a call up here. Nobody on the line to giggle with me as I describe a cartoon in my head of people wearing phones like snails wear shells. Sidewalks mobbed by see-through booths, each occupied by a person chattering away. Booths elbow for position like guys on the playground fight for a rebound or booths waddle-waddle-waddle by like young men of color, pants below their ass cracks waddle like toddlers with loads in their diapers. A few rare ones walk booths with old-school cool—sexy, macho, etc., but booths very difficult to maneuver, shaped a bit too much like upright coffins. Then Emmett Till's glass casket joins the mix and nothing's funny. Booths collide. Booths crush bodies contorted inside them. Booths burning. Apoplectic faces of trapped occupants, fists pounding glass walls. Riders dumped, mangled, heads busted, bleeding on the curb.

If I could explain whitespace, perhaps I could convince everyone down there to take a turn up here. Not that it's comfortable here, no reasonable person would wish to be in my shoes, I'm not even wearing shoes, tossed overboard with socks, sweatshirt, jeans, jacket, beret. Stripped down to skivvies and intermittent sunshine the forecast promised not doing the trick. Each time a cloud slides between me and the sun, wind chills my bare skin, my bones shiver. On the other hand the very last thing any human being should desire is comfort. World's too dangerous. Pulse of the universe ba-dup, ba-dup beats faster than the speed of light. Nothing stops, nothing stays, a blur of white noise. People, cities, whole civilizations wiped out in an instant, steeped in blood, obliterated. If we could see it, not a pretty picture. Ba-dup. Comfort never signifies less peril, less deceit, it only means your guard's down, your vigilance faltering.

On the bridge one dark day, thick clouds rolling in fast, sky almost black at two in the afternoon, I caught a glimpse of a man reflected in a silvery band of light that popped up solid as a mirror for an instant parallel to the walkway fence, a momentary but too, too crystal-clear image of a beat-up hunched-over colored guy in a beret, baggy gray sweats, big ugly sneakers scurrying across Williamsburg Bridge, an old gray person beside me nobody loves and he loves nobody. He might as well be dead. Who would know or care if he dies or doesn't, and this man scurrying stupid as an ant in a box, back and forth, back and forth between walls it can't scale, is me, a lonely, aging person trapped in a gray city, a vicious country, me scurrying back and forth as if scurrying might change my fate, and I think what a pitiful creature, what a miserable existence, it doesn't get any worse than this shit, and then it does get worse. Icy pellets of rain start pelting me, but between stinging drops a bright idea—universe bigger than NYC, bigger than America. Get out of here, get away, take a trip, visit Paris again, and even before the part about where the fuck's the money coming from, I'm remembering I detest tourism, tourists worse than thieves in my opinion, evil and dangerous because tourists steal entire lands and cultures, strip them little by little, stick in their pockets everything they can cart back home and exchange for other commodities until other lands and cultures emptied and vanish, tourists worse than thieves, worse like false-hearted lovers worse than thieves in the old song, you know how it goes, a thief will just rob you . . . ba-dup, ba-dup . . . and take what you have . . . but a false-hearted lover leads you to the grave. Tourists worse than thieves, like false-hearted lovers worse than thieves, but a false-hearted lover far worse than any worst thing you can imagine. So where to go, where to hide, what to do after seeing that ghost.

Once I had hopes love might help. Shared rapture once with a false-hearted lover. I'll start with your toes, my gorgeous lover whispered, start with your cute crooked toes she says, your funny crooked toes with undersides same color as mine, skin on top a darker color than mine she grins and when I'm finished with your toes she promises my false-hearted lover promises I'll do the rest.

Hours and hours later she's still doing toes, she's in no hurry and neither am I. Enraptured. Toes tingle, aglow. How many toes do I own. However many, I wished for more and one toe also more than enough. Toe she's working on makes me forget its ancestors, siblings, posterity, forget everything. Bliss will never end. I read *War and Peace*, *Dhalgren*, *Don Quixote* and think I'll start Proust next after I finish *Cane* or has it been Sonny Rollins's mellow sax, not written words, accompanying work she's busy doing down there. Whole body into it, every tentacle, orifice, treacly inner wetness, hers, mine. I'm growing new toes or does one original toe expand, proliferate, bud, bloom, breed. Could be one toe or many, who knows who cares, she's still at it and who's counting.

I floated miles above her, us, them, it, far removed from this "inextricable place," as a favorite writer of mine named the world. Time stopped—yes/no—then here it comes. I hear it whirring, starting up again. No. Nobody turned off the time machine. I just missed a beat. Missed one tick or tock and fell asleep before the next tick or tock. Time only seemed to stop, as during a yawn, blink, death, rapture, as in those apparently permanent silences between two consecutive musical notes Sonny Rollins or Thelonious Monk brew, or between heartbeats, hers, mine, ours. A hiccuping pause, hitch, an extenuating circumstance like being tickled by my mom while I'm attempting to act grown-up, dignified, serious.

Falling . . . slipped out of love. It's afterwards and also seamlessly before she starts on my toes and she's still in no hurry. No hurry in her voice the day that very same false-hearted lover tells me she's falling . . . slipped out of love.

Shame on me, but I couldn't help myself, shouted her words back in her face—*falling . . . slipped out of love.* Who wouldn't need to scream, to grab her, shake her, search for a reflection in the abyss of her eyes, in the dark mirror of whitespace. I plunged, kicked, flailed, swallowed water, wind, freezing rain.

Sad but true some people born unlucky in love, and if you're jinxed that way, it seems never to get any better. No greeting this morning from my neighbor ghost, not even a goodbye wave. Can't say what difference it might have made if she had appeared in her window. I simply register my regret and state the fact she was a no-show again this morning.

I believe it's her I speak to politely in the elevator. Her I nod at or smile or wave at on streets surrounding this vast apartment complex or when we cross paths in the drab lobby shared by the buildings we inhabit. When I moved into my fifteenth-floor, one bedroom, kitchenette, and bath, the Twin Towers still lurked at the Island's tip, biggest bullies on the block after blocks of skyscrapers, high-rises, the spectacle still novel to my eyes, so much city out the window, its size and sprawl and chaos would snag my gaze, stop me in my tracks, especially the endless sea of glittering lights at night, and for the millisecond or so it took to disentangle a stare, my body would expand, fly apart, each particle seeking out its twin among infinite particles of city, and during one such pause, from the corner of one eye as I returned to restore the building, the room, my flesh-and-blood self, I glimpsed what might have been the blur of a white nightgown or blur of a pale, naked torso fill the entire bright window across the courtyard from my kitchenette window, a woman shape I was sure, so large, vital, near, my neighbor must have been pressing her skin against the cool glass, a phantom disappearing faster than I could focus, then gone when a Venetian blind's abrupt descent cut off my view, all but a half-hand-high/thirty-inch-wide band of emptiness at the window's bottom edge, increasingly familiar and intimate as years passed.

What if she had known that today was her last chance. For a showing as in Pentecost. Jewish ghost to Gentile apostles, their eyes all a-goggle, flabbergasted, humbled, scared. Nobody's fault it didn't occur. No different this morning, though it's my last. Her final chance, too. Sad she didn't know. Sad she may have moved out years ago. Too bad I won't be around tomorrow to tell her I'm up here today so we can be unhappy about it together, laugh about it together. Her name, if I knew it, on the note I won't write and leave behind for posterity.

Posterity. Pentecost. With a phone I could review both etymologies. Considered bringing a phone. Not really. Phone would tempt me to linger, call someone. One last call. To whom. No phone. Nowhere to put it if I had one. Maybe tucked in the waistband of my shorts. Little tuck of belly already stretching the elastic. Vanity versus necessity. So what if I bulge. But how to manage a call if I had a phone and someone to call. Freeing my hands would mean letting go of the thick pipe/railing, an unadvisable maneuver. Accidental fall funny. Not so funny, not acceptable, not my intent. Would spoil my show. A flawless Pentecost this morning, please.

Posterity, *Pentecost*, old-fashioned words hoisting themselves up on crutches, rattling, sighing their way through alleys and corridors of steel girders, struts, trusses, concrete piers. Noisy chaos of words graffitied on the pedestrian walkway: *Dheadt Refuse—Eat Me—Jew York—Poop Dick Dat Bitch—Honduras.* Ominous silence of highway free of traffic as it never is except rarely after hours and even during the deepest predawn quiet a lone wolf car will blast across or weave drunkenly from lane to lane as if wincing from blows of wind howling, sweeping over the Williamsburg Bridge.

Why the most outmoded, most vexing word. Staggering across Williamsburg Bridge one morning, buffeted by winds from every direction, headwind stiff enough to support my weight, leaning into it at a forty-five-degree angle, blinded by the tempest, flailing, fearing the undertow, the comic strip head-over-heels liftoff and blown away—goodbye, goody-bye, everybody—and I asked myself why the fuck are you up here, jackass, walking the bridge in this godforsaken weather, and that question—*why*—drum-drum-drumming in my eardrums, the only evidence of my sanity I was able to produce.

Why not let go. Escape whitespace. Fly away from this place where I teeter and totter, shiver, hold on to a cold iron rail, thighs pressed together like sissy girls afraid of the dark, clinging, hugging each other for warmth and company, fingers numb from gripping, toes frozen stiff, no air in my lungs or feathers. If I possess feathers. If I possess wings.

Always someone's turn at the edge, isn't it. Aren't you grateful it's me not you today. I'm your proxy. During the Civil War a man drafted into the Union Army could pay another man to enlist in his place. This quite legal practice of hiring a proxy to avoid a dangerous obligation of citizenship enraged those who could not afford the luxury, and to protest draft laws which in effect exempted the rich while the poor were compelled to serve as cannon fodder in Mr. Lincoln's bloody, unpopular war, mobs rioted in several Northern cities, most famously here in New York, where murderous violence lasted several days, ending only after federal troops were dispatched to halt the killing, beatings, looting, burning.

Poor people of color by far the majority of the so-called draft riots' victims. A not unnatural consequence given the fact mobs could not get their hands on wealthy men who had hired proxies and stayed behind locked doors of their substantial mansions in substantial neighborhoods protected by armed guards during the civil unrest. Poor colored people on the other hand easy targets. Most resided in hovels alongside hovels of poor whites, thus readily accessible, more or less simple to identify, and none of them possessed rights a white man required by law or custom to respect. Toll of colored lives heavy. I googled it.

So much killing, dying, when after all, a proxy's death can't save a person's life. Wall Street brokers who purchased exemption from death in the killing fields of Virginia didn't buy immortality. Whether Christ dies for our sins or not, each of us obligated to die. On the other hand the moment you learn your proxy killed in action at Gettysburg, wouldn't it feel a little like stealing a taste of immortality. Illicit rapture.

If suicide a crime, shouldn't martyrdom be illegal, too. Felony or misdemeanor. How many years for attempted martyrdom. Neither a life sentence nor capital punishment would have deterred Jesus. Terrorists not deterred either. Was Jesus serving time on Rikers Island when Sonny Rollins showed up. Did they jam together.

Sitting here today folded wings heavy as stone I can still imagine how it might feel to fly. I can imagine whitespace parting as wings, strokes, words enter it and form stories with beginnings, middles, ends. I can imagine such stories being written and printed, imagine myself and others inhabiting them, reading them, imagine how memories of what's been said or written seem real, but I cannot imagine where whitespace begins or ends. White pages whir past and dissolve. Myself printed, my invisible colored ink pushed across blank space. Blind leading the blind.

When you reach the edge you must decide to go further or not, to be free or not. If you hesitate, you get stuck like the unnamed, fair-skinned, young colored man in Reisner's photos. Better to let go quickly and maybe you will rise higher and higher because that's what happens sometimes when you let go—rapture. Why do fathers build wings if they don't want sons to fly; why do mothers bear sons if they don't want sons to die.

On TV I watched the arm of a starfish float away from its body. The diseased fish captive in a huge tank in a lab so its death could be observed and filmed by scientists. Arm separates, glides away, leaves a hole behind where it had detached itself, a dark wound leaking vital fluids and fluttery shreds of starfish. Loose arm long and straight, slightly tapered at one end, a hard, spiky-looking outer shell, interior soft, saturated with suckers. Off it floats, slowly, serenely, as if motivated by a will of its own. I could have easily believed the arm a new fish foraging in the tank's flood-lit, murky water. Except an absolutely unimpeachable voice-over informed me the starfish is unable to regenerate lost limbs and a severed starfish limb unable to grow into a new starfish.

When I let go and topple backward, will I cause a splash, leave a mark. After the hole closes, how will the cops locate me. I regret not having answers, not completing my essay on whitespace. The plunge backward off my perch perhaps the last indispensable piece of research. As Zora Neale Hurston said, You got to go there to know there.

At the last minute for comfort's sake, for the poetry of departing this world as naked as I arrived, maybe I will remove these boxers. Why worry about other people's reactions. Trying to please other people a waste of time. At my age, I understand good and well my only captive audience is me. Myself. I. Any person paying too much attention to an incidental detail like shorts is dealing with her or his own problems, aren't they, and their problems by definition not mine. Allowing other people's hang-ups to influence my decisions gets things ass-backwards as the elders used to say. Perhaps people down below are my proxies—halt, lame, blind, broken-in-spirit, lost, abandoned, terrified, starving proxies saving me to live another day, ba-dup, ba-dup, buying time for me with their flesh-and-blood lives while I shiver and sway up here. Their sacrifices in vain, no doubt. I'm too close to the edge, too much whitespace to fall or fly or crawl across. I have no words to soothe other people's pain, to quiet their cries drum, drumming in my ears.

Can't seem to get underwear off my brain this last morning. Not mine, we're finished with mine, I hope. Though a woman's underwear in Paris, my undershorts today on Williamsburg Bridge surprisingly similar, both made of the same no-frills, white cotton cloth as little girls' drawers used to be. I'm seeing a lady's underwear and recalling another unlucky-in-love story. Last one I'll tell, I promise. A civil war precipitated by underwear. Not a murderous war like ours between the States. A small, bittersweet conflict. Tug-of-war when I begin pulling down a lady's underwear and she resists.

I was young, testing unclear rules, slippery rules because of slippery eel me. Civil war waged inside me by my slippery parts. I wished/wish to think of myself as a decent person, an equal partner, not tyrant or exploiter in my exchanges with others, especially women. Which meant that whatever transpired in Paris between a lady and me should have been her show, governed by her rules, but I was renting her time, thus proxy owner of her saffron skin, slim hips, breasts deep for a young woman. Why not play. Wrap a long, black, lustrous braid around my fist, pull her head gently back on her shoulders until her neck arches gracefully and she moans or whimpers deep in her throat.

I had asked her name and when she didn't respond immediately, repeated my French phrase—*comment t'appelles-tu*—more attention to pronunciation since she was obviously of Asian descent, a recent immigrant or illegal, maybe, and perhaps French not her native language. *Ana*, I thought she replied after I had asked a second, slower time. Then I shared my name, and said I'm American, a black American—*noir*—I said in case my pale color confused her. I asked her country of origin—*de quel pays*—another slight hesitation on her side before she said—*Chine*—or she could have said Ana again or the first Ana-like sound could have been *China*, I realized later. Her name a country. Country's name spoken in English, then French, an answer to both my inquiries.

Anyway her eagerness to please teased me with the prospect that perhaps no rules need inhibit my pleasure. I assumed all doors open if a tip generous enough added to the fee already collected by a fortyish woman on a sofa at the massage parlor's entrance on Rue Duranton. Only unresolved issue the exact amount of *pourboire.* I didn't wish to spoil our encounter with market-stall haggling, so like any good translator, I settled for approximate equivalences and we performed a short, silent charade of nods, looks, winks, blinks, fingers to express sums and simulate acts, both of us smiling as we worked, hi-ho, hi-ho.

I trusted our bargain had reduced her rules to only one rule I need respect: pay and you can play. Her bright, black eyes seemed to agree. Resistance, they said, just part of the game, monsieur. Just be patient, *s'il vous plaît.* Play along. I may pretend to plead—no no no no—when your fingers touch my underwear, but please persist, test me.

Easy as pie for a while. Underwear slid down her hips to reveal an edge of dark pubic crest. Then not so easy after she flops down on the floor next to the mat, curls up knees to chest, and emits a small, stifled cry. Then it's inch by inch until underwear finally dangled from one bobbing ankle, snapped off finally, and tossed aside. A minute more and not a bit of shyness. Time machine purrs, rolls on, da-bup, da-bup.

Wish I could say I knew better. Knew when to stop, whether I paid or not for the privilege of going further. Wish I believed now that we were on the same page then. But no. Huh-uh. Like most of us I behaved inexcusably. Believed what I wanted to believe. Copped what I could because I could. No thought of limits, boundaries. Hers or mine. No fear of AIDS back then. Undeterred by the threat of hordes of Chinese soldiers blowing bugles, firing burp guns, ba-do-do-do-do-do as they descend across the Yalu River to attack stunned U.S. troops, allies of the South in a civil war, Americans who had advanced a bridge too far north and found themselves stranded, trapped, mauled, shivering, bleeding, dying in snowdrifts beside the frozen Chosin Reservoir.

No regrets, no remorse until years later, back home again ba-dup, ba-dup, and one afternoon Sonny Rollins practicing changes on the Williamsburg Bridge halts me dead in my tracks. Big colors, radiant bucketfuls splash my face. I spin, swim in colors. Enraptured. Abducted by angels who lift me by my droopy wings up, up, and away. Then they let go and I fall, plunge deeper and deeper into swirling darkness.

Am I remembering it right, getting the story, the timing right, the times, the fifties, sixties, everything runs together, happens at once, explodes, scatters.

* * *

I will have to check my journals. Google. Too young for Korea, too old for Iraq, student deferments during Vietnam. Emmett Till's exact age in 1955, not old enough to enlist nor be on my own in New York City, slogging daily like it's a job back and forth across the Williamsburg Bridge those years of Sonny's first sabbatical. When I hurried back to Rue Duranton next morning to apologize or leave a larger tip, it was raining—*il pleut dans la ville.* No Ana works here I believe the half-sleep women on the sofa said.

I wish these dumb undershorts had pockets. Many deep, oversize pockets like camouflage pants young people wear. I could have loaded them with stones.

Before I go, let me confide a final regret: I'm sorry I'll miss my agent's birthday party. To be more exact it's my agent's house in Montauk I regret missing. Love my agent's house. Hundreds of rooms, marvelous ocean views, miles and miles of wooded grounds. One edge of the property borders a freshwater pond where wild animals come to drink, including timid, quivering deer. Stayed once for a week alone, way back when, before my agent had kids. Quick love affair with Montauk, a couple of whose inhabitants had sighted the *Amistad* with its cargo of starving, thirsty slaves in transit between two of Spain's New World colonies, slaves who had revolted and killed most of the ship's crew, the *Amistad* stranded off Montauk Point with a few surviving sailors at the helm, alive only because they promised to steer the ship to Africa, though the terrified Spaniards doing their best to keep the *Amistad* as far away from the dark continent as Christopher Columbus had strayed from the East Indies when he landed by mistake on a Caribbean island.

I know more than enough, more than I want to know about the *Amistad* revolt. Admire Melville's remake of the incident in *Benito Cereno*, but not tempted to write about it myself. One major disincentive, the irony of African captives who after years of tribulations and trials in New England courts were granted freedom, repatriated to Africa, and became slave merchants. Princely, eloquent Cinquez, mastermind of the shipboard rebellion, one of the bad guys. Cinquez, nom de guerre of Patty Hearst's kidnapper and lover. Not a pretty ending to the *Amistad* story. Is that why I avoided writing it. Is Williamsburg Bridge a pretty ending. Yes or no, it's another story I won't write.

Under other circumstances, revisiting my agent's fabulous house, the ocean, memories of an idyll on Montauk might be worth renting a car, inching along in bumper-to-bumper weekend traffic through the gilded Hamptons. My agent's birthday after all. More friend than agent for years now. We came up in the publishing industry together. *Muy* simpatico. Rich white kid, poor black kid, a contrasting pair of foundlings, misfits, mavericks, babies together at the beginning of careers. *Muy* simpatico. Nearly the same age, fans of Joyce, Beckett, Dostoevsky, Hart Crane (if this were a time and place for footnotes, I'd quote Crane's most celebrated poem, *The Bridge*—"Out of some subway scuttle, cell or loft/A bedlamite speeds to thy parapets/Tilting there momently"—and add the fact Crane disappeared after he said "goodbye-goodbye-goodbye, everybody"—and jumped off a boat into the Gulf of Mexico). We also shared a fondness for Stoli martinis in which three olives replaced dry vermouth and both of us loved silly binges of over-the-top self-importance, daydreaming, pretending to be high rollers, blowing money neither had earned on meals in fancy restaurants, until I began to suspect the agency's charge card either bottomless or fictitious, maybe both.

Muy simpatico even after his star has steadily risen, highest roller among his peers, while my star dimmed precipitously, surviving on welfare, barely aglow. How long since my agent had sold a major piece of my writing, how long since I submitted a major new piece to sell. In spite of all the above, still buddies. Regret missing his party, Montauk, the house. House partly mine, after all. My labor responsible for earning a minuscule percentage of the down payment, *n'est-ce pas*. For nine months of the year no one inhabits the Montauk mansion. In France vacant dwellings are whitespace poor people occupy and claim, my mother had once informed me. Won't my agent's family be surprised next June to find my ghost curled up in his portion of the castle.

Last time in Montauk was when. Harder and harder to match memories with dates. One event or incident seems to follow another, but often I misremember. Dates out of sync, whitespace conflates and erases everything. Except rapture. Rapture unforgettable, consumes whitespace. Sonny Rollins's sax squats on the Williamsburg Bridge, changes the sky's color, claims ownership of a bright day. Was I in fact walking the bridge those years Sonny Rollins woodshedding up here. I'll have to check my journals. But the oldest journals temporarily unavailable, part of the sample loaned to my agent to shop around.

I'm sure I can find a university happy to pay to archive your papers, he said.

Being archived a kind of morbid thought, but go right ahead, my friend. Fuckers don't want to pay for my writing while I'm alive, maybe if I'm dead they'll pay.

Stoppit. Nobody's asking you to jump off a bridge. Nothing morbid about selling your papers. Same principle involved as selling backlist.

So do it, okay. Still sounds like desperation to me, like a last resort.

Just the opposite. I tempt publishers with posterity, remind them the best writing, best music never ages. Don't think in terms of buying, I lecture the pricks. Think investment. Your great-great-grandkids will dine sumptuously off the profits.

Whoa. Truth is I've got nothing to sell except whitespace. What about that. How much can you get for whitespace.

What in hell are you talking about.

Come on. You know what I mean: whitespace. Where print lives. What eats print. White space. That Pakistani guy. Ana . . . Ana . . . la-di-la-di-da-da . . . something or other who wrote the bestseller about black holes. Prize client of yours, isn't he. Don't try and tell me you or all the people buying the book understand black holes. Black holes. White space. White holes. Black space. What's the difference.

Whitespace could be a bigger blockbuster than black holes. No words . . . just whitespace. Keep my identity a secret. No photos, no interviews, no distracting particulars of color, gender, age, class, national origin. Anonymity will create mystery, complicity—whitespace everybody's space, everybody welcome, everybody will want a copy. Whitespace an old friend, someone you bump into in the Houston airport lounge. Wow—look who's here. Great to see you again. Big hug, big kiss. Till death do us part.

* * *

The *Amistad* packed with corpses and ghosts drifts offshore behind me. Ahoy—ahoy, I holler and wave at two figures way up the beach. No clue where we've landed. I'm thinking water, food, rescue, maybe we won't starve or die of thirst after all. The thought dizzying like too much to drink too fast after debilitating days of drought. Water, death roil around in the same empty pit inside me. Faraway figures like two tiny scarecrows silhouetted against a gray horizon. They must be on the crest of a rise and I'm in a black hole staring up. Like me they've halted. I stop breathing, no water sloshing inside me, no waves slap my bare ankles, roar of ocean subsided to a dull flat silence. My companions stop fussing, stop clambering out of the flimsy rowboat behind me. Everybody, everything in the universe frozen. Some fragile yet deeply abiding protocol of ironclad rules, obscure and compelling, oblige me to wait, not to speak nor stir until those alien others, whose land this must be, wave or run away or beckon or draw swords, fire muskets.

The pair of men steps in our direction, then more steps across the grayish whitespace. They are in booths making calls. Counting, calculating with each approaching step, each wobble, what it might be worth, how much bounty in shiny pieces of silver and gold they could collect in exchange for bodies, a rowboat, a sailing ship that spilled us hostage on this shore.

My Friends, calls out the taller one in a frock coat, gold watch on a chain. His first words same words Horatio Seymour, governor of New York, addressed in 1863 to a mob of hungover, mostly Irish immigrants, their hands still red from three or four days of wasting colored children, women, and men in draft riots.

* * *

I'm going to go now. What took you so long, I bet you're thinking and maybe wonderingly why—*why* this moment, and since you've stuck with me this long, I owe you more than, *why not*—so I'll end with what I said to my false-hearted lover in one of our last civil conversations when she asked, What's your worst nightmare.

Worst nightmare. Good question.

So answer me already.

Never seeing you again.

Come on. Seriously.

Seeing you again.

Stoppit. Stop playing and be serious.

Okay. Serious. Very super serious. My worst nightmare is being cured.

Cured of what.

What I am. Of myself.

Cured of yourself.

Right. Cured of who I am. Cured of what doesn't fit, of what's inappropriate and maybe dangerous inside me. Cured absolutely of me, myself, I. You know. Cured like people they put away—way, way far away behind bars, stone walls, people they chain, beat on, shock with electric prods, drug, exile to desert-island camps in Madagascar or camps in snowiest Siberia or shoot, starve, hang, gas, burn, or stuff with everything everybody believes desirable and then display in store windows, billboard ads, on TV, in movies, perfectly stuffed, lifelike, animated cartoon animals.

Lying naked in bed next to naked her I said that my worst nightmare is not the terrible cures nor fear I fit in society's category of people needing cures. Worst nightmare is not damage I might perpetrate upon others or myself. Worst nightmare, my Love, the thought I might live a moment too long. Wake up one morning cured and not know I'm cured.

P.S.—the other day, my friends, believe it or not, I saw a woman scaling the bridge's outermost restraining screen. Good taste or not I ran towards her shouting my intention to write a story about a person jumping off the Williamsburg Bridge, imploring her as I got closer for a quote. "Fuck off, buddy," she said over her naked shoulder. Then she said—*Splash.*

EXAMINATION

Democracy is a form of government that permits anyone/everyone, man, woman, child to play loud music you don't wish to hear. Or play quiet music you don't wish to hear in places you don't want to be.

Democracy permits unprotected sex, and I enjoy it so I let it happen and here I am, I said to the medical person—not a doctor obviously—who seems to be listening. A technician, not a doctor, since the person in a white lab coat with the facility's name in neat blue stitching above the breast pocket appeared genuinely interested in what I was saying. Doctors pay only minimal attention to a patient's description of his or her ailments. Doctors know that showing too much interest in a patient's monologue might suggest that the doctor has not heard similar stories many times before and this lack of familiarity with a patient's case diminishes in patients' eyes the physician's authority. Subverts the purpose of a consultation. Who's the expert. Who's in charge here. Who gets paid.

I say barely any of the above out loud, then say either to myself or to the woman in the lab coat—One thing you learn walking along the edge of the sea as I often walk—there's no edge. There are many, many edges. Countless. Sea and land are separate and not. Always changing. Never the same edge twice. Endless edges. A paradox, a mystery you might consider, if such puzzles tickle your curiosity.

I listen to voices inside myself in the manner I think doctors (some technicians, too) listen to patients' voices. Though doctors get paid for sitting, nodding, and doing nothing while a patient rattles on, the real work doesn't start until a patient shuts up. So why do patients narrate long-winded versions of their stories. A patient a novel from a bookstore rack the doctor samples. No obligation. When patients talk too much, doctors ring the receptionist to send in the next person or call time-out for a toilet break or lunch or two weeks of family holiday in the Bahamas.

Democracy promised similar autonomy to ordinary citizens like you and me. The choice to pay attention or not. Respond or not. To ration our compassion, our identification with other people according to whatever public or private reasons we choose. The right to steer clear of ambiguous edges of other lives and harbor no secret motivation nor temptation to slip beyond our actual life. Beyond a single self. A sort of slippage clearly impossible anyway.

As if to shut me up and get real work started, a needle interrupts the conversation. Sorry, the technician says when I flinch. She had positioned my left arm—shirtsleeve rolled up, elbow bent, forearm resting on her desk—then tied an elastic band above my biceps, palpated my flesh to choose a vein, and promised,

Just a little pinch. Cool swipe of alcohol my last awareness of her presence before I had closed my eyes to drift outside myself or deeper inside and avoid the little pinch she had warned I would receive.

When you shut your eyes, miss, and the world vanishes, do you ever worry you might forget how to reverse the world's vanishing trick and be stranded in limbo forever. Maybe you glimpsed that worry in my eyes and assumed this guy's squeamish about having blood drawn. I'm not, miss. And you needn't apologize for performing your job, please. The poke you administered is a clever response to my riff on edges. A reminder how precisely, instantly a needle can locate a body's edge. An impeccable argument. I can counter only that blood circulates. Constantly moving like a sea. And being a medical person you know more about this than I do. Blood is body and body blood. Blood cells die and are born, a flowing, changing soup. Cells replenish the body as body replenishes cells. Time a factor. Time always is since it doesn't end or begin or at least we will never know how or when. Takes time for a needle to pass through blood that is body then body that is blood, layer after layer of neither blood nor body, both without being either, if you're following me. Many edges flickering past and you or I wouldn't believe a person possesses only one edge if we were tiny enough to ride the needle, see through its eye.

Certain constants, constraints may exist, I suppose. Situations or ideas or bodies confined within a stable boundary unlike the sea's infinite edges. Permanent divisions, arrangements, races, maps. Hierarchies. Homeostasis. Periodic table of elements. Laws, rules, chemicals, algorithms, golden ratios. Certain predictable combinations and permutations of numerical, logical possibility. Ineradicable essences. As a student of science you may be able to cite some.

Or perhaps not, the newer physics claims. Untruths inside Newton's and Einstein's truths. New speculations, dispensations aim not to displace totally those once unquestioned classical understandings of the material world but rather to offer alternative theories and explanations that imply any truth not truthful enough.

Like lies I tell my wife. Lies that brought me here. To be examined. To be treated if necessary. Or worse, to be informed I'm untreatable. A lost cause. Like all those other refugees, illegal immigrants, and migrants adrift today. Stripped of moorings. Edges collapsed. No way in or out. No illusions. No reliable language, family, country, money, clothes, name. No past except unpleasant memories of abuse, helplessness, hunger, war, dependency, labels and tasks that confined them from cradle to grave. No future unless a new set of labels and tasks drops providentially from the sky.

Still, the social instinct our most irresistible, irrepressible urge. Our need to fit in with others, fit them within our edges. The imperative that drives me to engage you, a complete stranger more or less, in conversation. Without the social instinct, wouldn't each individual's fear and selfishness, our relentless pursuit of individual survival undermine the biological imperative of our species to multiply.

Driven by the desire to multiply, we develop other mathematical skills—subtraction, addition, division—as well as the sciences of language and statistics to rationalize growth, loss, chaos, the escalation from individual to couple to family, clan, nation. We discover we are more and less. Not alone yet more alone. We pay doctors to listen. Examine.

When I examine the social instinct, I consider the meaning of words such as *duty*, *obligation*, *responsibility*, and visualize a tall, narrow, antique wooden filing cabinet. I pull out her drawer and my wife's inside it, miniaturized, perfectly believable. Gently I lift her out till she's stretched in the palm of my hand. She is peaceful. Aware there are no probes, no purges as part of the examination. Just my eyes running over her, missing nothing—expert, loving—and then I place her again on her soft, mauve pallet in the drawer. Drawer pushed back inside the cabinet notable for its craftsmanship, attention to detail. No change in her. No more than it would be reasonable to anticipate after all the years together, confined within, more or less, the same edges.

All edges socially constructed. That is the enlightened view today, and maybe you share it. Ideas, categories—water, earth, gender, wind, fire, color, etc.—that regulate, connect, and separate people are temporary, provisional, imaginary formulas. Why do these fictional edges we invent threaten as much as comfort us. Why don't they moderate fear of extinction. Serve us in the abyss where we touch nothing and nothing touches us. The abyss of extreme proximity with no contact. Proximity without touching because the abyss intervenes. It gets rid of everything, including what we make of ourselves, think of ourselves. The abyss as close as we ever get to knowing what comes next. And next a dead end. Nothing's there. Nothing's what our edges abut. Surprise and no surprise. *Abyss* even sounds a bit like *emptiness.* And *abyss* sounds like *miss*, doesn't it, miss. But abyss not us. Not anything. We learn to take it and we get it.

For over twenty-five years now we have constructed a dream—my wife's, mine, ours—of sharing a living space, a social space. Sharing the broken peace, broken pieces of our construction. We decide to take a trip and wind up thrown from our Volvo, bodies sprawled, unable to move or speak at the edge of a highway. Cars and trucks whizzing past and nobody notices our accident, peril, pain. Maimed, probably lying there in shock, but the traffic pays us no attention. If you are her or me you imagine dying. Or imagine yourself cured and attempt to stagger up. Or imagine an emergency vehicle brimful of miraculous lifesaving technology and kind, exquisitely trained technicians who will listen to your silence, heads bowed, ears close to your shuddering chest, flopping heart.

Title of a novel shivers irretrievable as most of my past as I try to recall it, then title appears—*Preparation for the Next Life*, exactly as printed on the paper cover. A book I'm recommending to you because—but not only because—I detect a trace of Asian ancestry in your features. An observation, miss, I hope you will accept as a compliment, especially in this small room with its lack of color, lack of history, its loneliness and intentional suppression of sociability so as not to disturb you or me or the doctor during the business of an examination. Anyway, the novel's two main characters—a young Chinese woman who's an illegal immigrant and a young American vet just back from Iraq—suffer a love affair in New York City. Love haunted by anger and madness, a love doomed as the Twin Towers. I was touched by their suffering, their determination to survive for each other despite brutal, anonymous energies of a vast city driving them together, thrusting them apart. A reader is immersed in violent, claustrophobic details of lives headed nowhere as the two lovers prepare for a next life. One that will never arrive, the book lets us know in no uncertain terms.

I, too, am an author of sorts. Fortunately, there are lots of people far smarter than I am who are not taken in, not deceived by what I do or call myself—by my fiction, my career, my words—yet they are deceived by what they do—math, physics, watching TV, taking photos, making families, money, minstrelsy, making love. Should that general failure serve me as any consolation. A reason to feel better about my limits, my edges, my failures to achieve, succeed, deceive.

Recently, on one of the long walks I don't really enjoy until it begins to feel interminable, I caught up with an ancient truck dumping stones to shore up the bed of a dirt path I'd followed five kilometers or so through woods and fields. A man in the truck's cab, girl on foot beside it, maybe the driver's young wife or his daughter, leveling with a shovel each new pile of white, chunky stones. Good day, I said smiling, and thanked them for their hard work, letting them know for aging warriors like me whose job is to keep the countryside free of demons and dragons, reliable roads a necessity, particularly back roads wending through thick forest, fields of tall grain, high weeds, and grass where ogres hide alongside the path or drop from overhanging trees to ambush passersby. Winter snow, spring rains will mock the couple's efforts as demons mock mine, but grizzled man, young woman whose arms and wrists seemed very slim for such heavy labor returned my smile, then waved after I overtook them and looked back over my shoulder.

Perhaps doctors listen in a reserved manner to conceal how appalled they are each time by the spectacle of a patient attempting with the immateriality of words to speak for the body's blunt, mute materiality.

Atticus, the given name of the author whose novel I recommended. Atticus also the name a Roman writer had assumed to celebrate being a citizen of Athens. During its golden age, Athens a cradle of democracy and civilization until it expanded its edges to become a state, an empire, then toppled as all empires and persons must. *Oh, how the mighty have fallen*, ancient Egyptians carved on their monuments, Greeks inscribed on their stelae, Yoruba expressed with imperturbable gazes of bronze masks, all looming brow curved like a full sail, designer lips thick, enigmatic as a Buddha's. *Oh, how the mighty have fallen. Oh . . . Oh, how beautiful the fallen.*

I understand there's nothing personal about this procedure, miss. Results must be objective, the social strictly in abeyance. You and I cease to exist during an examination. We are ghosts. Offstage, hovering in the wings. Irrelevant as far as data is concerned, data gathered, rendered into more data, more trustworthy than any person's opinion. Numbers that do not require us while they crunch out conclusions, predictions, solutions, results verifiable whether or not we're around. I've been here before. Inured to inconveniences—long waits, exorbitant fees, needles, knives. Still. Let me put it this way. Or rather, let me ask you a question, please. Do you share about any portion of your anatomy my secret squeamishness about navels. Gown pulled up, naked parts exposed to a stranger's eyes—no problem unless my silliness about navels kicks in. I squirm inside at the thought anyone may touch the site, the scar where once I was joined with another. A part of me severed. Cord cut, twisted, stuffed back into me. An edge of me never quite safe. Drastically vulnerable in fact. An ugly hole not filled completely. A pit sunken in fleshy lips through which things that belong inside may spill out, get lost again.

They say drowning's the easiest death. Somebody says it. Mermaids the only witnesses, maybe. Only a few moments of thrashing, flopping around, too busy to pay attention to that dreadful, instantaneous last review of your life they say you always receive, then water's over your head and your edges flow into water, water flows into your edges. The rest is drift. Peace.

Oddly enough, miss, though you may find it hard to believe today, I was not always an old man. No prostheses, prescriptions, wrinkles, no humiliating dependencies on professionals to keep me alive. Women—some—attracted to me. One exceptional one in particular who happened to be too good to be true. By that I mean not simply that she possessed unusually good looks and smarts. She confessed to being enormously enthralled by me, so much so that she was happy to do anything I asked with no expectations on her side of something from me in return. Too good to be true. She asked no questions about times we weren't together. No obligations, plans, excuses, explanations required. Please, she said, just be yourself and let yourself be pleased by me.

Circumstances (including my wife, kids—I'm endeavoring to be completely honest with you, miss) did not allow us to meet often and each rendezvous tended to be brief, though quite intense. Too intense to last, a reasonable voice inside me warned. Too good to be true.

Of course I anticipated disaster. Sooner or later my worries, guilt, and selfishness, her unselfishness and generosity would be punished. I couldn't conceal my anxieties and they hurt her. Afterwards and sometimes even during, Why do I sense you running off, she asked. Why do you doubt what we share. Why express dissatisfaction about a situation you obviously enjoy. Do you want what we have to continue or not.

I guess my answer no. Couldn't say this then, but I will admit it to you now, miss. My fear she was too good to be true the reason the affair ended. I spoiled it. A glorious gift turned into a threat, an omen, and I lost track, lost touch with our moments together not because they were too good to be true but because I wasn't prepared to treat them as true. Did I step back because I thought I saw the edge. Did I believe *true* possessed only a single edge. A self-fulfilling prophecy, wasn't it. Surely as night follows day, miss, I fucked up. Pardon my French, please.

You're getting very busy with papers, with opening and shutting drawers of your metal desk. Is the examination approaching a conclusion. Maybe not, since the voice telling this story doesn't require an audience, doesn't need your assistance, doesn't need you. It can rattle on and on whether you listen or not, whether I speak to you or only to myself. In its humble fashion narrative is too good to be true.

I'm not going to embarrass either of us by asking you for a date. I know all too well what time it is. How long it took to arrive at this facility, this moment it's your turn and mine to occupy.

Oh. Oh my, my. We all fall down. In spite of what we learn the hard way or what we overhear people say, hope does spring eternal. A woman twenty, thirty years my junior eager to do whatever I ask. An unlikely truth once. More than unlikely twice. A young woman eager to do my bidding, as people used to say. No. Not *bidding.* I retract that word. It's too old-fashioned. Reminiscent of emperors, masters, servants, slaves. No. Not about power, miss. Power not the point. It's the creeping seduction, the exhilarating experience of thinking, even in a field hospital grim as this one where wounded are transported to die, even here, anything's possible.

What notes have you jotted in my file, miss. Will I receive copies of pages you are tucking into folders of various colors spread like an oversize deck of Tarot cards on your desktop. Do you perform happy endings in this institution. What opinion do you have of my chin. My left leg. Ear. How much do I owe.

WAIL

Wail of sirens continuous. A woman coming from the direction towards which I hurry, her clothes sooty, in disarray, shouts at no one in particular. People are jumping out windows. Beneath the East River a subway from Brooklyn to Manhattan carrying my daughter to work may be trapped under burning buildings. My stepson's grade school only blocks from where war or the end of the world beginning. A man has rolled his black, shiny sedan up over the curb, turned off the motor, and sits, legs hanging out the passenger side door—nice shoes—radio behind him broadcasting full blast live updates from the site where planes are smashing into the Twin Towers. Driver wears an expression I'd seen in a movie once, on the face of a blue-coated trooper huddled behind the rump of a dead horse shot out from under him by waves of Sioux arrows. Sirens wail nonstop that day and I still hear them.

Of course one can always say afterwards, after the shock of death passes, that we knew it was coming. But still we remain stunned. Still we must admit we were unprepared. Not prepared to survive. Better at preparing the dead. Ancient rules, rituals, techniques in place to prepare the dead for separation. Release them from obligations to the living, from consorting with the living. These practices we've organized to free the dead from the burdens of those who survive are generally satisfactory. Or at least seem to be since the dead don't complain. No equally reliable protocols prepare the living. Whether a death long anticipated or sudden, ask any person who survives the loss of a loved one if measures taken to prepare for separation were satisfactory.

The living left behind unprotected. Not sealed underground in wooden boxes or marble or cremated or interred in catacombs. For the living, the dead's absence confuses time. Confuses our sense of who's present and not. Absence of the dead true and false. A theft of time. We lose track of before and after. Does someone missing today remain gone or return tomorrow. Or both. Is it yesterday when the missing one returns. Disappearance of the dead a fact and not a fact. Line drawn in the sand by the living that the dead may choose to honor or ignore.

The dead's removal provokes silent exchange. Silence the first rule, first word, next word, every word of conversations with the dead no one living is prepared to undertake. Until it's too late. You're in the middle of one and it never ends. Except, of course, you understand that sooner or later it must. And know how.

You will never not be astounded by how quickly, how far the dead are able to travel. How instantly and adeptly the missing one navigates vast space utterly alien to you, and how again and again you must accept the truth that the lost one, or rather the one who is not lost but found elsewhere, belongs there, belongs *elsewhere*, so seamlessly, totally, that you begin to wonder how you could have believed this place, this *here* exists. This place you and the one lost to you once seemed to share.

You can't get used to it. That distance. That speed that separates. That unexpected terrain the dead reach. Where they fit. Where you don't fit and fit. A place which seems as impossibly far away for the lost one as it is for you. Though there you both are.

Do you remember me

I think so

Who has broken through. Who is finally speaking.

Better not kiss me, she says. Not there, anyway. A sore on my lip, she says. Here, she says and offers a pale cheek.

LINES

In spring the leaves turned red, nobody remembered anyone else's name, executions were scheduled, a line formed outside the prison's wall. Lines form, said the lady famous for her book about lines, lines form, she wrote, when/because something's lost or something found or someone wants something or someone doesn't want something—and although all reasons lines form are analytically classifiable into these four basic categories, any particular line, whether at Lourdes, Bank of America, or outside a prison, is likely the product of mixed motives, she argues quite convincingly, with examples of lines she's stood in, seen, heard of, imagined, or researched in archives. Her line schema unchallenged finally, referenced inevitably in any serious discussion of lines, as lines themselves are inevitable in a world where people find and lose, desire and don't, wait for executions to begin or end inside the walls of a prison they stand outside, no recourse but to form orderly lines as directed by uniformed guards and troopers who seem to outnumber those in line, until a line grows too long to see the end.

We were on our way to join the line outside a prison's towering stone walls. Decided after driving all day to stop at a motel near our destination. A good night's sleep to refresh and fortify us. We'd be in line early next morning. Soon enough, we both agreed. Stopped. Made love before dinner as if the next day had already dawned, and we had secured a place in line, and had to hurry back in line before our absence was noticed.

I did not share with my companion of the moment a feeling I had stayed once before in this motel where we have stopped. Stayed here on a trip with my former wife. Neither the coincidence of a previous visit nor my unhappy memories of my wife should spark anyone's jealousy. Except the woman I am with plagued, like me, by fierce competitiveness, vanity, and insecurity that empowered her some days and on others struck her impotent, cowering in dark entanglements she weaves about herself. No matter how disturbing an ancient trip and recollections were for me, the woman I'm with would be angry, desolated, probably stay awake fretting all night, if she learns I had stopped here with my wife or learns that while I lay beside her dreaming tonight in one of this motel's beds, my ex might appear.

Nothing about the motel's reception area particularly familiar when we arrived, but I recognized immediately the manager at the desk as the same one who checked us in many years before. Was it his face that triggered my recollection of a previous stay. Or had I remembered the motel earlier that day on the road and decided to return. No way to be sure whether my decision to return conscious or unconscious. Either way, a guilty choice I couldn't deny as soon as the manager's eyes met mine.

He knew. But aside from that fact, his expression unreadable. How much could he know. He must be a local, nailed down here.

I wondered why he hadn't closed the motel and joined the line. Would I see him over there outside the prison tomorrow, busy registering names. Would he ask for my name again.

While the woman accompanying me showers before she comes down for dinner, same man serves me a drink in the motel's tiny bar/restaurant—three stools, brief counter, a few tables and chairs—crowded under a staircase to Level 2. Once I'm planted on a stool I keep reminding myself not to stand up too abruptly and to stoop slightly when I move from under the alcove's overhang to greet my lady.

Like quiet rain falling in a city never visited before can transform that city's foreignness into intimacy, the man's bluntly African features, deep color, his accent remind me in spite of the passage of many years, he's familiar. I had not forgotten him. He putters, chatters as he pours me a drink, pours one for himself, raises his glass in the direction of mine for an imaginary bump. What does he remember of our last meeting decades ago. Not my diluted color, diluted features. My eyes, hair, lips, nose betraying my origins as a medley of a little bit of this, a little bit of that. A guy who appears at this motel on a second occasion and displays unchanged his taste for a white woman. Or two. Same woman or different. Would the man notice.

Cheers, I say. Ask if he remembers me.

I believe so, he says. Yes. Of course. As you recall me. But sorry, not your name, though you just said it to me a few moments ago checking in. My name, by the way, Simon. Simon-Kimbanga-

Mpoyi-Kitawala-Feruzi-Kudjabo-Ndjoli-Mobuto-Kelenge-Katadi-Tshibamba-Kasavubu-Lumumba . . .

All that.

More. More. Names are strands of cloth wrapped round us, round the earth so everything doesn't shiver and die of cold. Names wrap round and round and round.

He refills both stubby shot glasses. My ancient uncle, he says, who claimed to be over two hundred years old, told me stories about names when he was in a certain mood, almost a kind of trance you could say or better call it a twilight zone between way back then and now. Way back then meaning, I assume, years when the uncle was a boy and his country still a colony, and even further back when old men of his village were boys before his country a colony, before it was anything in stories told to village boys who became elders and told them to the uncle, anything other than the sole place in the universe where gods saw fit to teach humans how to suckle at the tit of life, where gods whispered instructions that became more people, birds, trees, animals of the forest, became wind, water, clouds, mountains, words, stories, news his old, old uncle passed on to him he passes to me.

But now, I respond. Today. Where are all those words, stories, names. Now when enemies crush and shred us, piss on us. Or string us up to the tops of poles. Fly us like flags without countries in the prison yard.

* * *

Same old uncle also said, he says, that the past reappears, not disappears. Different and same. Like your name when it's said by someone who speaks a foreign language. Same and different. Like grass and weeds sprout through the motel's gravel driveway no matter how much I kneel and pick, pick, pick . . .

Man behind the counter offers me the motel or at least his job managing it in exchange for my place in line the next day. Offers to take my woman, or at least one of my women, he smiles, to accompany him while he occupies my spot in line. What do you have to lose, he asks. Who will miss you. Blame you.

I'll be stuck here alone.

No. No. Not alone. Guests arrive. Surprises. Lines of them sometimes stretch to the horizon.

NAT TURNER CONFESSES

Nat Turner no stranger to me. The grad-school education I'd been privileged to receive in the early 1960s included an American Studies course which mentioned slave revolts and named a few slaves responsible for bloody, short-lived, essentially futile outbreaks of violence that occurred before Lincoln's Emancipation Proclamation and the Civil War ended legal slavery in America. My curiosity led me to discover a handful of radical, left-wing scholars who specialized in uncovering and preserving evidence of slave resistance to bondage. Thanks to the research of those scholars I learned more about Gabriel Prosser, Denmark Vesey, Nat Turner, etc., and rebellions they had perpetrated. More information, of course, piqued my curiosity for more. But not the kind of curiosity that killed the cat. My good liberal education was also instilling moderation. Instructing me how to divide and conquer. Conquer and divide myself first. A very large, unforgiving, ruthless world out there and no one—especially some lucky someone like me who had been granted a special pass to enter places reserved for people not my color—could afford to squander time and resources on projects leading nowhere. Except to the dead ends of history, to dead people buried in the rubble who had wasted their lives in hopeless quests.

Nat Turner addresses the spectators with silence. A goodly number had turned out to see him hanged and he is pleased. The more of them shivering under a slight drizzle this dismal morning, the easier it is for him to say nothing. Easier to wish he'd begun the work of killing them sooner, these strangers and the few he might recognize if he cast his eyes about the throng, dark faces here and there among white faces he's sure, the ones ordered by masters to attend this edifying spectacle, or dark faces peeking curious, wide-eyed, pretending to be invisible at the edges of the crowd, and though he blinds himself to it, he hears and smells the mob fragrant as the pig yard where someone not him, thank goodness, must be shoveling mud and shit already at this hour. A rabble boiling around the hasty scaffold, this cross erected in a farmer's field just beyond Jerusalem. So many white faces it's easier to forgive himself and his band for not completing the work of eliminating them all, every single one, as he'd conceived in his plan and exhorted the others, returning in one instance to a ransacked dwelling, strewn with corpses of a family they had just murdered, to bash in the skull of an infant girl he remembered they'd missed in an upstairs nursery. One by one, every single guilty one of them, man, woman, child slaughtered until he and his recruits had emptied Southampton, Virginia, the entire world, or until they, themselves, cut down.

Not a word Nat Turner desires to speak to anyone today, not a person he wishes to see, only the dead, his loyal troops who did not survive, scores of innocent folk, men, women, children rounded up on plantations, from village streets, swamps, woods, and rumored to have paid with their lives for his sins, the Emmetts and Trayvons murdered as if guilty of riding with Nat Turner that August night of killing, and yes, oh yes, speak a last word to his poor wife beaten unmercifully until she produced, they say, "odd papers written in blood" then stripped and whipped again, as if a flesh-and-blood woman whose husband long a ghost to her could reveal his whereabouts, as if her naked flesh privy to his secrets. Sorry, sorry, he might whisper to his lost bride, to those victims he served.

Then Thomas Gray intrudes. Not his face picked out from the crowd. Thomas Gray's gray face not seen from the scaffold this last morning. He's invisible as the other spectators, invisible as I had been while he read my so-called confession to the court at my trial. Confession Gray had written himself and claimed that I, the accused, had dictated to him. Gray's lying voice heard again here in this moment of truth, the moment people say no one dares violate with an untruth because death imminent, and we fear God's all-knowing stare.

I would relish an opportunity to watch the eyes of Thomas Gray—my inquisitor, lawyer, judge, jury, priest, executioner as he variously styled himself—watch his eyes consume letter by letter, word by word, not the counterfeit confession he authored. Watch him pelted by the witness I bear, the truth of this unfolding tale I compose to occupy myself during these final minutes while I stand beneath a gallows fitted with three hooks and ropes, standing above a mob that now mutters and seethes as it grows more restless, impatient because I say nothing, my lips stones, though I believe, in the instant Gray meets his creator, he must listen to every word I brew now, words scourging him, words streaming, stinging up from my belly to my heart to my silent mouth this morning.

May Thomas Gray hear my confession, not his. My words. Not the words he's written and intends to publish for great profit, a businessman like others in the crowd who wait for my body to be cut down so they can strip patches of my skin, chunks of my flesh and peddle them as Christians once peddled splinters of the true cross.

As a boy I learned to read. Taught myself names of letters, sounds of letters that are also their names. Learned the alphabet: A–Z.

A = an apple. Apple bitten ends darkness. Animals wake up to light which is another dark. Animals see what they have never seen before. See themselves and see one another and it's the beginning of the end. A–Z. Alone. Not alone. A–Z begins with first taste of A for apple. First open eye. First glimpse of what a world is. What a person is not. World holds others like you and unlike you. Creatures with nothing to do with you. Separate. Like rivers, trees, mountains, sky, snow, a bird, shadows. And everything not you burns, roars loudly or silently. Creatures hungry, hunt, haunt a world beginning and ending with the alphabet that begins with letter A. Ends with letter Z.

B = Book = Bible. Be. Bee bee busy bumble bee. Buzzy, fuzzy, striped B for bug with wings, stings, hives, honey. To be in pain. b. To begin to read the Bible letter by letter because each letter a sound, the world an empire of sounds buzzing in your ears, noises people make, world makes. Bee crawls, slow, striped black and yellow, and you catch it in your fist, listen, crush, squash it. No buzz. Before it was a bug, a bee, but nothing now, even when you open your fist, open your eyes, only darkness. Read dark, darker, darkest. Bible opens to letter A, to letter B, alpha to beta, A–Z, I read somewhere and learn to sound out names for god, suckle at the alpha-beta tit, listen to blood-red, white milk squeezed up sweet inside, singing inside warm pillow of skin, sometimes it puts me to sleep, wakes me up in the deep, down darkness, deep quiet again—being alone with only God again—still as a squashed bug, squashed b—it's not Him, not me, not it—broken—but, because many, many Bs—busy, busy b's—b b b—you could spell a world with nothing but b. Beginning begotten baby born black butt big boy bigger better best blest bought beaten beast behave beg blind until he learns C, the next letter, and learns next, and next creature, because black boy learns (A–Z) to read God's Book.

C: See with eye. C sounds like see. Eye sounds like I. Eyes C. I see sounds like *icy.* Icy makes you slip and fall. Feet up over head. Head down under feet. Happy little white girls and boys bundled in bright, happy colors skate on ice in Lil Miss book. What is ice. Ice cold, dummy. White, smooth, slippery ice. You slip and fall and fall, if you not careful. Boom down you go. C, I told you so, dummy. Crack your noggin. Hard head nigger noggin. I told u so. U better b careful. Or when you C eyes first time you fall. What is ice. Not nice. White, white eyes everywhere, cold, colder, coldest after dark, after sun goes down. No ice here, see, c, it's there in picture book, God's snow and tall mountains and his children in bright colors fast as deer, his cold ice and hot sand of his deserts you will never see, you sleep, fall asleep and darkness wakes u, u C, eyes see pictures in books with pages u cannot turn, pages turning too fast, too slow, pictures with no pages your eyes see. Icy. You slip and fall. See nothing. Eyes cold white as God's ice everywhere.

D for Dread. Dream. Did. Dirty. Deed. I did it. I admit I did. Fucked her, yes. Did it, but swear I'm not happy or proud I did it. Swear she said okay. Not all slave masters enjoyed screwing their slaves. Whipping slaves. Slavery, yes, a terrible, terrible institution, I admit it, and we all agree, but still not all masters the same. There were good guys and bad guys. Bad apples but some decent, too. Not everybody roots for the same team. Always winners and losers. Heroes and goats. Why shouldn't I be a winner for a change. Me, Nate Parker, and my underdog, underground railroad team. We did it. Made a Nat Turner movie and everyone promises it's a hit. On top for once. Let me tell you it hasn't been easy. Making a movie not a cakewalk. Not one easy step along the way. And not easy now. Even now after a winning score in the book declares me a winner. On top at last. Free at last. Film in the can. Hand in the till. Here, let me sprinkle some this honey money on your tongues, my brothers. No fun all these years being exploited. Called bad or evil or flat-out ignored. But if you are willing to forget and forgive, I am. We can go from here. New start. New season. Put the bad times behind us. What's over is over. And done. Let's put that bad stuff out our minds. I'm willing if you are. New day. New game. What makes America great, the game great, is it not, my sisters and brothers of all colors. Thank you for this opportunity. This chance to perform. Said I was sorry, didn't I. Didn't Mr. Gray read my confession. Can't you hear my sobs of remorse. Let bygones be bygones. Let's all us be free at last. Why lynch me now. Won't bring back the dead. We got our whole history in front of us. Let's do it, Maceo. Give the drummer some. Let the good times roll. Promise youall I'll be a good boy. Hardest worker in showbiz.

E: With about forty Es lined up in a row, a long chain gang of Es maybe different sizes, shapes, colors, letters strung out one after another, would the sound of all those Es make the sound of a mule you might hear dawn or dusk mad cause it's tired, hurt, broke, pissed, weary, tired of being whipped, winded, trembling at the knees, long mule neck aching so bad, not one more mule step left in skinny mule legs, emaciated mule muscles, nothing left to do except squeal eeeeeeeeeeeeeeee till the final mule breath exits its mule-assed body, mule-assed soul. Eeeeeeeeeeeeeeee.

F: Father. Fast, flee, freedom, friend. Fount of wisdom. Foundation. Founder. Fire, fear, flee, feast, famine. Father forgive. Flay me. Fly me. Far, far away.

G: Only one sound, one letter, and I am unworthy. They say I am forbidden to utter, to spell it—only G. No other letters. Only an empty space after G___ for my God's name.

If you believe you already know my story, perhaps you should stop here. The story you know suffices. You will discover nothing useful in what I have to relate. Nothing that will raise doubts or supplant truths or untruths inside you that you have transported until your life's journey progressed to this point where you find me offering my alphabet, my tale, my confession as if it begins here, gushing new like pure water from a pristine mountain stream, when both of us, though we speak separate languages, understand the fact my life, like yours, has been unraveling a long, long time and we are both past the point of going back or starting over, strangers in this moment we might prefer to be a moment of truth, strangers to each other and ourselves as we pass by, as we exchange words weightless as strangers passing by.

Sad day yesterday.

Heavy day, sure enough.

Lil Miss coffin didn't weigh much. Mize well be feathers in there.

Not carrying a coffin what I'm talking bout. Talking about tears. All that crying. Ole Missus and them so sad. And fixing to rain all morning before we dig that hole put the box in the ground.

See. You just didn't want get wetted up. Fraid your black ass gon melt it get wet.

Know what you can do for my black ass, nigger.

Turrible day. Turrible sad, what I'm saying.

Not your mama in the box. Nor your daughter they sold away last planting season.

I decided to kill white people when the voice I hear sometimes in my head reasoning with me said you don't need them. Need no one to tell me I am not one of them and never would be. Don't need masters. Do not need the heaven and hell in their churches. Nor the hell on earth they make of this Virginia. Don't need fellow slaves. Nor slave rags and slave rations and slave quarters. Don't need nasty sheep to tell me I am a nasty goat and don't belong in the sheep pen.

I found it strange then, since I had been persuaded, agreed wholeheartedly, I thought, with the voice of reason, strange that once I had commenced the killing, strange that at first, each time my turn to strike a fatal blow, fear or panic or pity or something else I have yet to fathom, caused me to hesitate. Standing over the bed of sleeping Joseph Travis—appropriately our first victim since he was owner of the plantation on which I, leader of the plot, resided—I struck him several times with a hatchet, but Will's assistance necessary to dispatch him. When I attacked Miss Newsome with my sword, Will's implacable ax was required again to deliver the fatal blow. In the side yard of her family's dwelling,

Mrs. Margaret Whitehead grabbed my hand and pleaded, but I struck her numerous times with my sword, causing her to collapse to the ground, though she didn't die until I snatched up a loose fence railing and crushed her skull. Were these mishaps the result of small, inadequate weapons, or my novice's ineptitude at killing. Or did I hesitate, temper blows in each instance, because I still believed if I eradicated them, I might miss the presence of white people.

I am called Nat Turner, a name made up for the convenience of sellers and purchasers of me. A made-up name like I invented a name for the voice inside me, calling it God's voice when I endeavored to describe the source of words no one besides me able to hear. Though that source, I must admit, far beyond my poor wits to fathom and remains impossible for me to explicate, I tried with all my powers to share the words of the source with my brethren in chains. Attempted to convince them that if they listened carefully to words that seemed to issue from my lips, they would hear more than Nat Turner speaking. Prophecies and mysteries would descend upon all of us when we gathered in secret places in the woods.

WHITE PEOPLE DO NOT CHANGE. WILL NOT CHANGE. SO THEY HAVE CHANGED YOU. WROUGHT YOU—BENT, TWISTED, EMPTIED YOU—TO BE WHO YOU ARE. ARE YOU SOMEONE YOU WISH TO BE. OR SOMEONE WHITE PEOPLE WISH YOU TO BE. YOU ARE INSIDE THEIR PLAN, NAT TURNER. BUT NOT INSIDE THEM, NAT TURNER. THEY ARE INSIDE YOU. REMOVE THEM. REMOVE YOURSELF FROM THEIR PLAN.

* * *

I began life with a mother and father. Like everyone does. Like you, like Mr. Thomas Ruffin Gray, I started with an Eve, an Adam. Though Eve and Adam not my parents' names, just conveniences I'm making up, like the name slavers fabricated for me. My mother's and father's names lost and forgotten long ago. The names they happened to bear when I was born had been passed out like tools passed out to field hands to serve their masters. Name to distinguish one piece of livestock from another, a name obliging you to come when it's called and face dire punishment if you don't respond quickly enough, names to shame or make fun of our condition, names stamping us as belonging to somebody, somebody's property branded with a name not connecting us to our mothers, fathers, sisters, brothers, ancient blood families preceding us in time, names erasing kin we are supposed to, taught to forget, names like mine, Nat Turner, who as far as I know never possessed another. Nor a family in whose bosom I was secure, protected as it was said white people we slaved for guarded their offspring.

Nevertheless, I was an extremely fortunate child. Still inside my mother's belly when she was ordered to the big house to serve Mrs. Travis and wet-nurse the infant Mrs. Travis expected. Extremely fortunate that after a baby everybody called Lil Miss born to the Travises, I was born, too, and accompanied my mother daily to the big house where she waited upon Mrs. Travis—suddenly Big Miss or Ole Miss or Ole Missus behind her back—and nursed the new daughter with whom you might as well say I shared a birthday.

My mother, less fortunate than me, told me, You two babies long wit everything else I had to do just bout killed me, boy. Said she carried us two, one on either hip, one at either titty, she said youall alike as two peas in a pod, except one pea white, other pea black and my mother smiled when she said it, and said young and strong as I was you two wore me out said too much work to do around the house, always more, chore after chore, kitchen, nursery, them two older chillens needing me, scrub, tidy this room then that and you babies hanging on to me mize well be twins, twin trouble, double whining and double hollering and double wet and stinky and sick and mischief, and running off and hiding or fighting or into something you ain't got no business being in soon as the two of you large enough to get up on two legs or four legs you could say, my, my, the two of you had my poor head spinning round trying to keep up, lay you down at night, my son, then dropped down myself like a dead person on that mat in the little closet kinda room behind Ole Miss Travis room lots of nights but seem like quick as a person could say Jack Robinson one or the other of you screaming in one or the other room, then both fussing and it's starting up again weary as I am it's starting again and Ima tell you the God's truth you two little devils just bout killed me and Ole Miss all laid up in bed all whiskey-headed and mumble bout this or that nothing or laid up under her soft sheets and wool blankets snoring never lift a finger to help.

They say Lil Miss made funny down there.

Say no babies

Say husband say he gon send her back to her daddy's house

Say Ole Miss say you got her, keep her

Say the husband beat her like a dog, hurt her bad like he beat his people

Say his people say he turrible mean
Say listen at you, fool, they all mean
Say Lil Miss not mean
Say uh-huh and Lil Miss dead

When you fall asleep in another person's dream, what happens if you awaken. Where are you. Who will you be. Have you become the dream's dreamer. The Dream. Perhaps you awaken and see yourself sprawled like one of her rag dolls Lil Miss props up to imitate the way she sits when she pretends to read, or perhaps she copies a doll sprawling in a corner, crumpled, soft, head drooping, wide-apart legs and butt resting flat on the floor, or knees steepled, seamed white cotton crotch exposed, back leaned against the wall, sitting so she appears alive reading or dead or asleep, you watching, waiting for her to scold and chase you away or coodle-coo and say come play.

We were children. Two of us growing up alone, many, many hours, most of most days and some nights spent together. Curious children. We looked at, touched, tasted each other. Playmates. Curious children. Play-named each other. My mother's duty to care for both of us daily. Blackee. Missee. My mother occupied by other duties, left us to fend for ourselves at an early age. No, no, no, Mrs. Travis hollered at my mother, her peer in age and both about to give birth. No daughter of mine raised in the nigger pen full of little dirty niggers. No. You bring yours here to keep her company.

Many hours. Many days alone. Children together. Curious. Learning. Uncovering secrets. Inventing games, names. One mother busy, busy. One mother absent. One burdened with way too many duties. One burdened with no duties. We were children left alone. Explored secret patches of yard outdoors, secret patches of rooms indoors. We learned every inch, inside and out. Every hidden hiding place. Laughed, tickled, scratched, whispered. Shared secrets. And when tired or bored or outraged we fought like beasts. Screamed. Sulked. Sullen. Made up riddles so the other one couldn't know the answer. Teased. Hurt each other. Licked. Pinched. Sniffed each other. Children growing inside each other. Away from each other. Girl. Boy. One of us could be both, or be the other one or chase away the other until the other missed too much by both, until the other returned and we could be one again.

As a convenience—like the convenience of naming slaves—in order to shape the telling of my story and to deliver my confession in the most convincing fashion, I could name that period of my life before the great and total separation demanded then and now, the separation of children into different kinds and different worlds, I could call my first four or five years on earth "Eden," except to borrow that name for any time or place in Virginia would mock both Bible story and mine.

Blackee. Missee. Children. I watched her squat and pee. Nap. Weep. Ash on your black legs, she said. Nasty, ashy white. Go away. Or said, "Sulphur." Never heard that word, I bet, dummy boy. Devil smell. Preacher Wilson said it's Devil smell. Sulphur. You stink like the Devil, natty. Go way, you dum-dum dummy, boy. Stinkee, Sulphur boy. No. Come over here, nattykins. Let me lick your round black pot of belly. Tummy boy. Boy tummy with a little sprouty root down there. Weedy sprout. Not like nigger sprouts, nigger bare bottoms in the fields. Bare black asses under long shirts. Bend over show their bottoms. Bend over chopping weeds, grass. Show their business. Show long, rooty nigger legs. Long knives chop, swing back and forth, back and forth. Chop grass, weeds, cotton. Blades swing, swinging like Nanny used to tie us a swing on a low branch and swing us back and forth. Low branch above low roots running along the ground, roots popping out the ground like old, twisted gray old Devil fingers. No hair, no weeds around your tiny rooty little hair down there. Not like grown hairy niggers. Not like my mama. My father I seen him, too. See. Come here, scaredy-cat. Mama dead drunk look like she sleeping she dead as a dead frog. Look, Blackee. Don't be scaredy-cat. See me touch her, see, Mama's black black bush. See I touch it. Dare you. I see your big white eyes looking. Go on and touch it. Look at all that black nigger hair dead as a dead frog, natty, touch it, dare you touch it. Someday mine growing black like her. Promise I let you touch mine. Let you sleep in it, let you live in my dark patch, natty-boy.

Somewhere before the age of five or six, as they used to do things and will continue doing forever would be my guess, the great separation prevented me from accompanying my mother to the big house and I was assigned endless, mindless chores each day, chores to keep me busy, keep me with all the other little niggers in the little nigger yard or pigpen or garden, barn, outhouse, chicken coop, manure pile, garbage pit, etc. Anywhere except the big house. No errand, no question or urgent need for my mother served as an excuse to go anywhere near the Travis dwelling. A few scoldings and beatings clarified the dangers, the price of breaking the rule. Soon I was a boy large enough to go chop down forests, drain swamps, dig out stumps and boulders to clear fields that became new land where we would sow, cultivate, reap, and harvest white people's crops, a perpetual round of labors which profited others and kept niggers possessionless, hungry, poor, dependent, evil, exhausted. One day someone told Mr. Travis, Nat Turner can read, and I confessed to him and he tested me, discovered not only was I literate but could write and cipher. You are a peculiar one, Nat Turner, he said, finally, and a peculiarly smart one and steady, too, a hard worker, the overseers tell me, and I'd be a foolish businessman not to take advantage of your skills, to waste you on nigger work, wouldn't I, Nat Turner.

Little by little, step by closely watched step, I found myself assigned new tasks that required me to be decently dressed and reasonably clean of field muck and stench, tasks performed in the big house under the scrutiny of Travis, who gradually put more and more trust in me until I was more or less his jack-of-all-trades assistant (not immune, however, from occasional episodes of nigger work) summoned daily to receive a long list of chores, though very different chores than those my mother had complained almost killed her, but chores that kept me constantly occupied, like her, sunup to sundown and many hours more. By then, during my apprenticeship as clerk, overseer, buyer, seller, manager, etc., learning to fulfill impeccably the expectations of Travis and on my good days even anticipate them, Lil Miss was long gone, naturally, from the big house I frequented.

With a burnt black end of stick I had practiced writing letters of the alphabet on my palm. If caught, one hard swipe, rub against my shirttail or trouser leg and no evidence. Just a dirty nigger hand like nigger hand supposed to be dirty. Dark ash shows well on pink palm of hand. Easy to trace letters there. My hand not a large hand, not small, a middling size for a middling-sized fellow like me. Middling size hands, feet, and the rest. Good enough, I think. No hand big enough to fit the whole alphabet. Even drawing letters with a point not clumsy as the nub of stick. How many letters fit if I practice smaller and smaller, I wondered. If letters small enough, how many words might fit on my palm. If hand bigger, letters smaller could my palm hold a book. How many words in a book. Did I know enough words to fill a book. How many words could I spell. A book is many words spelled correctly with letters of the alphabet to make sentences, make sense, make a book. If I could spell many words correctly and write them with smaller and smaller letters, how many books might fit on my palm. Books so small, how would anybody read them. But if I wrote the letters, words, books, tracing them on my skin, wouldn't they be there whether anybody else able to see them or not.

Look, Nat, Mr. Joseph Travis said. My eyes obey and fasten on a brightly painted wooden ball, recently purchased, hollow inside as a dried gourd. I can detect the seam gluing together two halves of this globe, as Travis calls it, gripped by an iron claw that allows it to rotate atop a black iron pedestal in this room he calls a study. This ball a map of the entire world, he confides. This globe you're looking at, Nat, holds every place on earth—England, Italy, China, France, Rome, America. Brings every place on earth here for us to see in this room in Southampton, Virginia, where we stand. A round map of the known world. North Pole. Africa. No place missing. Almost magical, isn't it, Nat.

Both my hands, as if tied together at the wrists, are behind me, invisible to Travis. The globe too large. Too much of it for a runaway's feet to flee. Too much world to fly across to freedom. Fingers of one hand tighten, crush all the countries. All the white people inhabiting them, all the people wearing black, yellow, red skins, gaudy colors like the painted globe wears. Squeeze, crush until the map, the miles, people, the globe shrink small as a kernel of corn in my fist. I can throw it away or put it in my mouth and chew it, swallow or spit it out. This small, round world large enough to hold a master's study, this room in which Travis speaks and I listen, both taller than the globe Travis spins now atop its black iron pedestal. Travis taller than me as he rotates the globe and talks, talking as if he owns it, understands every place on it, this room with two men in it, his dwelling with its cellars, porches, shutters, columns, portico, stairways, attics, kitchens on a slave plantation, the map large enough to hold me, hold every alphabet letter, every word, and small enough to fit on one of my palms.

I refuse to believe the globe. No magic. No map. The North Star—God's cold, bright eye—only map a runaway should trust. Distant as it seems, that faraway light also inside, leading, guiding, all the map required to escape earthly bondage.

Show me my footprints on this globe you purchased. Where do the quarters fit. The chains. How could every shifting grain of grit or sand or puddle of pig shit under my bare toes be repeated here, preserved, doubled exactly, once and for all, but then again and again as it spins, here like mountains, rivers, clouds, animals, leaves, leaf by leaf and all leaves growing, dying over and over on a globe holding this room, this land holding us and being embraced in turn, Virginia a convenient name for a place holding this house, the silence, order, and tranquillity of this moment

I can hear Travis yearning to hold, embrace, celebrate, to sing a little praise song inside himself about this place, about this precise present moment, as if he could, as if he were a singing type of man, though he isn't, though in the silence I can imagine hearing him sing, as if he could, and I imagine Lil Miss propped up in a corner of wall, legs spraddled, mouth moving, pretending to read a book before she could read, before we helped each other learn. Travis praising the globe he rotates, his fingertips giving more a glancing caress than hitting the empty shell's wooden skin to keep it turning, Travis silent now so he can listen as if there's a song in this room coming from his lips.

I lean a ladder against a chimney behind the house and will climb it, step through a window into the bedroom where Travis sleeps. The day is August 21, 1831. I've known how to read since I was a boy. Taught myself at an early age clock time, calendars, how to write the name Nat Turner, the name Joseph Travis of the man who claims to own me, whom I intended to kill the past spring but I took ill, so will kill him today, August 21, 1831. Him first, then every other plantation owner, their women and children, relatives, white minions from here to Jerusalem. Perhaps when our work completed, I will write their names in a ledger. A thick black ledger to save names of whites murdered tonight, and runaways, and those who die trembling with fear of us and disappear into thin air. We must cleanse the countryside of them because we no longer require white people to tell us what to do, tell us our names, the hour, day of the week, month, year, color of our flesh.

Until we rid ourselves of them, until they are gone, we will not truly cleanse ourselves of the belief that we are nothing without them.

With each step up a ladder leaned against the back chimney's stones, rung by rung, I feel my feet rising higher, closer to freedom. Still, surrounded by night's darkness and silence, afloat, suspended as always between one instant and the next, when I enter the window open against August's sweltering heat, when my feet are planted on a solid wooden floor, will the first blow of my hatchet prove fatal. Or will I hesitate, temper the blow because I'm still afraid I might need white people. Nowhere, no one without them.

What's Egyptland, natty-boy. Niggers sing Egyptland when they sad, sometimes sing it happy. My blanket my Egyptland, little nat. Wraps it round me at night. Rub my nose with a corner when I suck my thumb. Smell my sweet blankey, nat-nat. Egyptland in it. Me, you in it.

No, you say. No-no. Stinky, you say. How dare you. Get your black ass over here this instant. Get over here and bend over. Take your beating, bad, bad boy. Say yes. Say sweet. Say Egyptland.

Ole Miss sent for me and here I am standing at the foot of her bed. Does she remember me. Does she know she will die asleep in this same room adjacent to her husband's while we dispatch him. Who is this large boy, I hear her eyes asking herself. No. I'm grown now. Man-size. No. Not man. Boy. Because if boy her girl still lives. This black something, standing here eyes lowered, mute as a mule, thick as a mule. Stink of him filling the room or is it already full she's asking, her dank flesh, hot breath reeking, room crowded with stench of death, sick vapors rising off wet, rumpled bedclothes. She is not afraid of dying, except if she dies, how will her poor baby find her, her poor lost girl wandering, haunting dark corners of the room: I'm back. I'm here, Mama. Where are you.

Who sent you here, you black imp. To mock me with your "condolences," your white word in nigger lips. You know better than to enter my bedroom. Someone put you up to this. A meddler. A fool.

You say I sent for you. "Summoned," you say, minstrel man. You grinning pillar of salt. You Devil mask. Why would I ever "summon" you. Your presence an abomination. Here where I grieve. Reminding me God took her and let you live. Breath in your body belongs to her. Stolen from her. As you stole her time. Why does God let your heart beat while hers has stopped. If I could snatch your bloody beast heart from your chest and plant it in her, I would. I detest you, Nat Turner. Your hateful presence reminding me she's not here . . .

Oh, Nat. Pitiful Nat. And pitiful me. If only I could take you like a baby in my arms. Hug you close to me. As if it would bring her back. Please. Please, go away. Let me die. Leave me my empty peace. My oblivion. My mother's grief. Make my child alive again, Nat Turner. My baby. Oh, let me touch you. Let me hug.

I could have begun this confession by speaking first of my father. With my time for telling stories almost over now, with a bloodthirsty mob milling around me, I regret I have not talked more about him, with him. I must admit—chagrined, ashamed—that I know very little about him aside from my mother's stories, mentions of him by my brethren in recollections they exchange to entertain one another. I'm able to put a face on gray Thomas Gray, but no face for my father. Except perhaps a shadowed version of my colored face. Yet at a crucial juncture when I needed to gain my brethren's trust in order to go forward with my plan to liberate us all, I called upon my father, used my father to allay their suspicions and doubts.

I confess today I again need his name. To steal his name. Be him. As if his name bestows his determination, clarity of purpose, ruthlessness, refusal to turn back and accept failure. My story could not exist without his. No promise of freedom, no uprising, no bloodshed, no record of violence released or violence suppressing violence, no numbing sense of futility, no guilt without him. Without the denial, the silencing of him.

A father, of course, part of a story you know already about me. No person on earth begins life without a father's seed. I could have started my story there—with his undeniable presence, but a presence slavery's evil constantly denied so that when I attempt memories of my father, I can only recall times he was absent. Father separated. Father withheld. Father embodied in words, thoughts, not a flesh-and-blood father. Father a runaway, a fugitive before I reached my fourth year. Runagate who escaped and never returned, never seen again.

My father must have been strong-minded and probably accumulated much wisdom and many practical skills he began perhaps to pass on to me before he ran away. I will never know what kind of man I might have turned out to be with him beside me daily. I am certain I inherited his strong back. They say a brother of my father was whipped to a whimpering pulp by an overseer's slave lackey and lay bleeding in a cotton field miles from the big house. Overseer said, Leave the nigger, but my father begged please, please, let me carry him, and overseer didn't stop my father from kneeling and slinging his brother over his shoulder and trudging all those miles back. But like Lil Miss returning to her father's house after what everybody said was a miscarriage, my daddy's brother dead when he arrived.

At the point it was necessary to enlist them, I began to share with my brethren my plan to seize freedom for us all. At first Will, Hark, Henry, Nelson did not trust me. Nor my plan, nor the spirit voice I claimed instructed me, nor secret meetings in the forest, nor my sudden enthusiasm for freedom. My initial four recruits—court would call them "co-plotters"—proved loyal, brave to the end. Despite their initial misgivings and mine. They had long been accustomed to regarding Nat Turner as odd—a solitary, private one who maintained a distance from his fellow sufferers, one who unless conveying orders from the big house seldom spoke, waited for others to start conversations. I worshipped differently, was rumored to speak to voices no one else could hear. My privileges and small property were resented. My seeming intimacy with Travis compromised any prospect of intimacy with them. Perhaps most disquieting and inexplicable was the fact I had been a successful runaway, then returned voluntarily to servitude. How could they trust a man who had spurned his own precious freedom.

Obviously, my plan required soldiers, so I was desperate to regain my brethren's confidence. Used my father. Most knew he was a runaway, a true runagate who had fled, disappeared, never seen again. I told them my mother had shared stories of my father with me. His promise to return at night and steal away with wife and son he dearly loved, she said. As a young man I had waited, anxiously anticipating the great day, the dark of night when he would arrive and carry us north to freedom. Gradually, I grew impatient—I explained to Will, Hark, and the rest—and became a runaway like my father.

Had no notion, I told them, of where I was headed, of what might lie in store for me, but whatever transpired, I assured them, I knew I was seeking my father. Wherever he abided, no matter how far away, no matter under what conditions, no matter what had prevented him from returning for us—captivity, dangers, even death—I believed I could run, run, run and one day I would join him.

Didn't find him, I told them. My father had vanished into a howling wilderness, so to speak. I was a fugitive, heart full of despair, loneliness, disappointment, and my sorrow, my yearning drove me back here. Here to reunite with my mother and wait for him again.

Thus, my brothers, in my fashion, I'm still seeking him here where my father has walked the land, cleared forests. Only here could I listen to my mother's stories, to stories in which other people recalled him or others like him. Here where he'd sowed and reaped, tended beasts, drank the water, smelled the air, wept for missing family, friends, sang the old songs you and I still sing together, I said to them. I stayed on this so-called plantation waiting, waiting, though part of me remained a runaway, runagate like my father, at liberty, no one's property, waiting until a voice announced, Now's the time, a new burning day of both darkness and light.

The voice speaks to us now. A fire burns, now, this very moment. Wait no longer, the voice exhorts, you must rise up, body and spirit. You, all your brethren. Reason together, rally together, the voice demands, now, today. All of us—men, women, runagates—we must seek out our fathers, mothers, daughters, sons, enslavers, murderers, strangers, ones loved, ones hated, invisibles, accused, accusers, prisoners, jailers, ourselves, the forgotten, forgiven and unforgiven, the forsaken and, Oh what a morning, Oh, what a meeting it will be, the old song promises, song we still sing, singing as we seek.

My confession ending now as it started. Alphabet letters (A–Z) spelling my story, telling it (A–Z). Ending. Beginning (A–Z).

EMPIRE

By now Empire has sorted out the sole distinction that truly matters—whether citizens are Givers or Gratefuls—and prohibits reference to specious categories (gender, race, religion, nationality, etc.), which had once differentiated and divided humans into warring camps.

Today a crew of Gratefuls can feel free to halt work and sprawl gratefully in the shade to consume their daily rations—bulky, pulpy pills they chew and swallow—grateful for energy the pills replenish, dry pills that miraculously brew liquid inside their bodies as a substitute for water, water long inaccessible to Gratefuls and rumored extinct. Pills generously distributed to all pods of Gratefuls each morning and night so no Grateful starves or dies of thirst or is lonely when a Grateful's turn to rest while other Gratefuls labor. *Waste Not, Want Not*, printed in large, bright-blue letters on each packet of pills, an admonition probably addressed less to Gratefuls than to Givers, since the skill of reading a lost art among Gratefuls.

Gratefuls talk. Talk their gift, their delight, the source, some Givers say, of perhaps too much pride—that endless talking all Gratefuls adept at from birth, it seems, silently conversing with their devices. Bowed heads hide their faces, conceal emotions that must be streaming constantly across their features as they engage in unspoken conversations, fascinated by whatever they see or punch into devices inexhaustibly patient, inexhaustibly responsive with infinite reams of pictures and games to provide answers to silent queries, devices that enhance or chide or channel endless curiosity Gratefuls appear to possess about something. Curiosity so insatiable, it's said, they exercise it even during sleep, their dreams operating as efficiently as their devices to animate silent conversations.

Each Grateful no doubt profoundly grateful for privacy which silence ensures, privacy bestowing license to say whatever they choose to themselves, no matter how outrageous or shy or absurd or irrelevant or lazy or daring or malicious. Or to say silently nothing at all if they choose. Generous license granted by Givers, just as Givers grant moments of pause, of leisure to Gratefuls to sprawl tranquilly in the imaginary shade of treelike art that lines a road they are cleaning, a road itself art, a decorative imitation because no use for it except to encourage Gratefuls to believe. To daydream that roads might lead elsewhere and that Gratefuls are able to go there.

Gratefuls grateful for the gift of art. Gift of pretending that ironclad connections forged by the Givers do not forever lock place to place, task to task, person to person, person to device. Why would anyone wish to believe imaginary work or imagined words soundlessly spoken into a device might actually construct a different Empire than the only one necessary and true.

By now we all accept the fruitful exchange between Givers and Gratefuls as permanent. As permanent as the way time moves. Time that's eternal though also different, moment by moment.

Like expressions that play across a Grateful's face while it talks to a device. Or like, Givers say, rivers that used to rush past in those days when rivers were common, rivers flowing constantly, never the same water twice. Never still, changing always.

Though once upon a time, Givers warn us, a Grateful, ungrateful for tasks assigned that day, mistook the daily exchange with Givers for a river that is always the same river, same water stepped into last time, stepped into every time, and cursed sameness with a grimace. That Grateful's face, emptied momentarily of its smile, broadcast invisible words almost loud enough for another Grateful nearby, who happened to be idle at precisely that nanosecond, to believe it had overheard. A grumble it tried to hear again in the other Grateful's eyes. As if by gazing at another's eyes it might see what its own eyes see when they watch the living and the dead. Living and dead who move faster than the speed of light. The living, the dead, the light dancing then disappearing into utter darkness that moves swifter than anything.

Grateful eyes made to open and shut and mind their own business and sleep and welcome darkness, but the Grateful searching for a grumble in another Grateful's face, started to wonder how it might feel to be lost or found in the other's darkness, the other's conversation, to feel another's device throbbing in its hands, another's ghost whisperings in its brain. And that wondering confused it. But not for long. Because, as Givers say, life is not long, and in the case of both confused Gratefuls, the usual allotment of life cut even shorter when the curious one communicated to its device a desire to experience again another's grumble. As if a grumble could form again, bright and blue as letters on packets of seeds.

As if Empire wouldn't intervene.

YELLOW SEA

Did you see *The Yellow Sea.*

First time I watched I was in bed and *Yellow Sea* unsettled me. Couldn't fall asleep. Googled reviews to keep myself company. One mentioned Truffaut's desire for movies that express the agony and joy of making cinéma. Several noted *Yellow Sea*'s homage to *Taxi Driver.* One reminded me Travis Bickle the name of the cabbie Robert De Niro plays in Scorsese's film. Plenty of information, but no review told me why sleep wouldn't come after I watched *Yellow Sea.*

In *Yellow Sea* a half-Korean, half-Chinese taxi driver who lives in China smuggles his young, pretty wife across the Yellow Sea to find work in Korea. She doesn't return, and the desperate, heart-broken driver crosses the sea to find her. Dies trying after a series of bloody, violent encounters with gangsters and cops. A thriller chosen randomly to be a sleeping pill, but it turned out to be a movie like *Precious* and keeps me awake.

Did you see *Precious.*

* * *

Yellow Sea and *Precious* are like the bubbles with words inside that began to appear right before a black girl set herself on fire and burned up in the street.

Did you see the girl burn.

A terrible thing to put on TV, but they did and how could anybody not look. One of those rare sights, rare moments life stops because you stop thinking about what will happen next. All the information you will ever need right there in front of your eyes. Too much in fact. Much more than you want, but you know you better not miss any of it. A black girl burning in the street is your life on fire. Beginning, middle, end in an instant. You are a shadow that wiggles inside the flaming pyre of her. The two of you are *dancing*, a word you try not to think but think anyway. When the girl finishes *dancing* she will be gone, her world over and maybe yours, too. Nothing could tear your eyes away from the screen.

She shudders as she washes herself in gasoline. Gas pools at her feet. Big butt splashes down in it. Miracle in all that wetness of a dry matchbook, a dry match and it strikes perfectly first time, last time, every time. Huddled shape of her shivers. A large, dark girl inside flames. Fire shrinks her until she keels over and she's gone. Gone like the cabdriver's wife. Like those monks in saffron robes in Vietnam. Like the taxi driver splashed into the Yellow Sea. Later you ask yourself, ask friends and strangers, *Where were you.* Not where were you during replays like replays of the Twin Towers on fire, buckling, collapsing again and again on TV. Where were you when she was alive. Alive once and burning to death.

During the week before the black girl burned to death, bubbles had begun to glide across the sky. Large cloud-like bubbles remarkable as the movies *Yellow Sea* and *Precious*. Those films remarkable in their way as the bubbles. At first only a few people noticed transparent clouds passing by with words inside. Then rumors became viral awareness. Imagine capsules in comic books floating above heads of animals or human beings to indicate they are talking and thinking. Or picture fluttering banners of words—a new movie, a Bible verse, bargains at Kmart—towed by blimps or prop-driven planes flying just above the tallest buildings. Except banners I'm trying to depict required no aircraft, no strings. A mystery how words stayed aloft. As mysterious as their source. Though some of us knew Jimmy Baldwin, author of many of the messages.

Clouds temporary as those tiny bubbles of air that rise and pop on a pond's surface. Clouds with words inside that pulsate and dance yet remain the same. Words visible from anywhere a person happens to stand as a cloud passes. Passing by slow enough for the slowest, barely literate readers to sound them out or popping, disappearing as quickly as swift readers peruse them. Same cloud doing same work for everybody. Efficient as death.

A month or so ago during my regular walk or jog along the East River, I was confronted by a mini-billboard mounted on a dolly with fat, stumpy tires. *Wanted for Sexual Assault/Black Male/Light Skin/17–25 Years Old.* A phone number at the bottom to report suspects. Bubble/clouds affected me like that sign. Reminded me of immense power surrounding me, power misused, abused far too often these days, so I decided to terminate my walk and hurried to the local precinct to complain. Insisted that I needed to speak to someone in charge, not fill out forms, and eventually a Lieutenant Orasco arrived. I demanded immediate removal of the blinking billboard. Its message dangerous and offensive, I said. A classic instance of racial profiling. Instead of aiding an investigation, the sign would further alienate fair-minded citizens of all colors from the police. Shaking his head, Lieutenant Orasco dismissed me and my assessment. Information on the billboard accurate, sir. So what's wrong, sir. His eyes flashed the same challenge as his words, but I was already out the precinct door, wondering who I could convince to help me roll the dolly to the iron fence bordering the river and hike it over. Imagining the splash.

Instead of more attempts to describe cloud/bubbles, here's what was inside the first one I saw:

EMPIRE NEVER INTENDED THIS TESTIMONY
TO BE HEARD

Only two words inside the next one I noticed:

PRECIOUS LOVE

And seeing that cloud like hearing an old gospel song.

I had met a Precious in *Precious*, the movie bearing her name, about a very large, quite dark teenage girl, unloved, unprotected by her mother, abused by a father who gave her AIDS and two babies. Whether or not we've seen the movie, all of us who live in this vast city encounter everywhere, every day, girls whose names we probably don't know who look like Precious. Some of us acquainted with a Precious. Some of us love or loved by a Precious. Some are Precious. Anyway, I steal the name and give it to the girl who burns in the street. Point being if a girl possesses a name and we know it, maybe less chance we will forget or forgive.

Over and over we watch the girl burn on TV like we watch a president shot again and again in Dallas. First the girl smiles shyly into the camera, shivering as she slops gasoline all over herself. Puddle forms on the sidewalk, and she plops her supersize booty down in it. Sits buddha style. We hold our breath each time, waiting for the match. If we know her name, perhaps we can get her attention. *Precious. No-no-no, Precious. Don't do it, Precious.* You can almost hear the match strike before you hear a loud *Whooussh* as fire explodes. Fire snatching her. Tongues of flame leap, lap, lick, snap, whip. Precious in the middle of dancing flames.

So much of her, big and black as the child is, a long time burning. How long. Too long. Too sad. Warning label pops up on TV, but who could shut off the set or turn their eyes away.

IF I HOLD MY PEACE, THE VERY STONES WILL CRY OUT

It wasn't the words in the air that finally brought us into the streets. It was Precious burning. TV called it a riot. Said woogies rioting because ghetto woogies have nothing better to do. Said it was drugs. Thugs. Drums. Said woogies copycatting African and Arab woogies tearing up their own countries couple springs ago. Said greedy bankers. Said woogies like to burn each other up. Said not enough prisons, not enough cops, too much welfare. Said it was because a man our color in the White House.

WANTED THE WORLD TO SEE
WHAT THEY DID TO MY BABY

Those words I saw in a cloud not Baldwin's. They were spoken by Emmett Till's mother, Mamie Till, as she stood beside a glass-topped coffin that displayed her son's mutilated face.

I want the world to see what youall did to me, said Precious, when she stepped down off the movie screen and set herself on fire.

Riot, or whatever it was, starts when a handful of mad, sad woogies pile into the street. Then bucketfuls of black woogies and some white woogies, too. We stop traffic, break store windows, turn over cars, set fires, liberate shit. Wave signs, torches, lynch ropes. Holler and scream for blood or peace or war or love or food or respect. Demand whatever it is we don't have and want and understand quite well we are never supposed to get. Time for a change is what we shout. Way past time, if truth be told. And change got to start with biting the hand that claims to feed us. Hand that fed poor Precious to death.

Whole lot of us out in the street that day got burned up almost as bad as poor Precious. We had waited too long. They were ready for us. Licked their chops. They had tanker trucks to spray us with nerve gas. Choppers to lay walls of fire from flamethrowers strapped like dildos up under their potbellies. Cops in blue helmets, SWAT team cops in ski masks, cops inside armored personnel carriers. Half the peacekeepers whose color I could make out colored like me so it hurt worse when they ran over us, ground our flesh and bones to brown oatmeal running alongside bright red blood running in the gutters.

After a while you couldn't see shit out there. Just smoke. Just sirens and glass breaking, niggers running, hollering, tear gas thick as Alaga corn syrup. As if we need more tears. Like we ain't been crying our eyes out twenty-four-seven ever since we got kidnapped and dumped in this wilderness. Rivers of tears. Rivers of blood.

Brother come flying past me swore he took down one of the peacekeepers. No doubt about it, he shouted, his PLO head rag trailing over his shoulder. Big ole gorilla, he said, but got my Lil David stone up under his blue helmet. *Splat.* Split his blue nose, blacked both his blue eyes, drew blue blood. *Splat.* Sucker won't be stealing people's blues no more.

Storm of stones flying like we used to fly Frisbees back in the day at sit-ins and march-ins on college lawns. TV says so much progress today the colored ex-president's kids and nice colored wife got Frisbees, a cute dog, their own large green lawn to play on. Hope they do. Hope they got every damn thing in the whole wide world they desire. TV says some people deserve it all. Might as well be some of us, right. Far as the rest of us concerned, we ain't got shit. Got nothing. And no damn body deserves nothing.

* * *

That's why we out here, Precious. What they did to you, what you do to yourself, dear heart, exactly why we are out here dying.

> *AN EMPIRE AT THAT MOMENT WHEN NO ONE ANYWHERE ANY LONGER ASPIRES TO THE EMPIRE'S STANDARDS*

What would a real Precious think watching a movie about a girl very much like her, a very heavy, very dark teenage girl with AIDS, two babies by her father, a girl who learns to read and write in order to better her life like the taxi driver's wife in *Yellow Sea* crosses the water to Korea to better hers. In the darkness of the theater would a living, breathing Precious wolf down popcorn and candy. Suck up rivers of soda through a straw. How is she dressed. Who's babysitting her very young, very ill kids. If the theater Magic Johnson's in Harlem, not the multiplex in Union Square where I first saw *Precious*, would the colored crowd's responses be in sync with what Precious feels as she watches. Would people signify, sigh, amen, cheer out loud like in the good old days at the Apollo. Is Precious disappointed at the end because the colored audience files out quietly, goes home to bed. Does she wonder why they don't sweep her up, all the pounds and pounds of her up on their shoulders and bust through the movie-house walls. Dance her through the Harlem streets.

Imagine an audience of *Precious* composed solely of big, dark-skinned, poor, unwed teenage mothers. Are they ideal spectators. Would they laugh with real Precious at parts she thinks funny. Or would they sit still and silent. Brood. Hide from start to finish.

When the houselights come on and they unstuff themselves from seats way too small for large bodies, will they chatter or avoid each other, these dozens and dozens of dark, overweight girls. Would each feel trapped in a theater full of look-alike images of herself. Feel outed, betrayed and ridiculed by a crowd of bodies indistinguishable from hers. Big, brown bodies exposed to entertain the mean eyes of others not her size, not her color. Would the necessity of negotiating rows and aisles crowded with bodies stunningly similar but each one obviously not her provoke the same sense of familiarity, the rush and claustrophobic terror anyone might feel watching a film of themselves on the big screen.

Imagine an audience comprised entirely of Joseonjoks—people of part-Korean, part-Chinese ancestry—watching *Yellow Sea.* Or watching *Precious.* I've read that Joseonjoks not really exactly welcome in either China or Korea. Mixed people divided like me by division and mixture and sorted into a category that often produces communities mired in poverty, no jobs, separate, segregated, plagued by crude violence, fear, coercion, and misconceptions. People forced to swim in a veritable sea of shitty, yellowish muck in which many drown. I am the taxi driver in *Yellow Sea* lugging a pregnant woman's bulky package up steep, outdoor, wooden stairs of a teeming tenement. Raise my fist to proclaim my Joseonjokhood. Hurry back down to my cab to rescue Precious.

JUNBI-HANI-DUL-SET-SIJAK . . . a cloud counts down in Korean. The taxi driver in *Yellow Sea* returns to China in a boat he hijacks from Korea. An ancient, white-haired sailor steers the boat. Watches silently, patiently as his passenger bleeds and loses consciousness. Then the sailor dumps passenger into the sea. But that's not the movie's end. In *Yellow Sea*'s final scene the cabdriver's missing wife, suitcase in hand, reappears. Surprise. Surprise. No sign of her since she left for Korea when the movie began, now here she is walking through a deserted, eerily quiet train station. Her young woman's flesh-and-blood body spectral as the ancient boatman and boat. Is she arriving or departing. What is she bringing or taking away in her bag. Why did she vanish. Where has she been. Is the story ending or starting up again. Where is the cabdriver. Who got drowned in the Yellow Sea.

In my movie about a real Precious in attendance at a film depicting her life, I seat myself next to her. She's not a ghost behind me in a ghost Chinese cab. Not a shadow gliding across the screen. She's massively here beside me in the dark. I sneak looks at her. Sniff her perfume. Does she notice me. Is she curious about my life. Is she sniffing me. Does she hear in a row behind us the young white woman's sobs I recall from my first viewing of *Precious* in a Union Square multiplex. Or is Precious too busy with her own story, holding on to herself and letting go of herself as image succeeds image in thin air right before her eyes. Her up there. Her story. Precious and not Precious.

Sometimes I believe parts of a movie and disbelieve absolutely other parts, but the unfolding melodrama can still get to me. Overwhelms. Certain moments too believable. Too real. Stir up too much anguish, foolishness, anger, madness. I have to laugh sometimes during *Precious* as I laugh sometimes during *Yellow Sea* to keep from crying.

Does movie Precious really believe she could steal a bucket of chicken from the counter of a fried chicken joint and outrun her pursuers. Maybe better to snatch a wing, darling, or a drumstick. Who couldn't catch you, Precious, if they seriously wanted to catch you. Your slow, ponderous body out of breath, wheezing after you walk half a block across the hood. How far you think you'd get haul-assing with a whole bucket of greasy chicken tucked under one heavy arm.

And that white chick in the mirror, mirror on the wall of your closet of a room. You don't even think she's that cute, do you, Precious. Plenty of fine colored women you'd dream about becoming before you'd dream you're her, right. Don't you scorn the airhead blond foolishness displayed by females who look like her in soaps, movies, sitcoms, ads. Don't you hate her contempt, the superiority of her gaze addressing you over counters of department stores, offices, ignoring you as she sashays her flat ass past you on downtown sidewalks.

And what about those light, bright, think-they-cute colored boys you daydream. Nice work if you can get it, maybe, but why would you bother with those knuckleheads, Precious. You know better than to believe a word the punks say. You know their yellow skin makes them no whiter than you, and you surely understand, don't you, girl, that your fantasy of hip-hop Hollywood/Bollywood stardom must always end with ceilings and skies crashing down on your tender head.

To survive day by day, my actual Precious, please tell me what resources of intelligence and spirit you deploy. Do you laugh, cry, talk to anybody, Precious. Scream, dance, argue with yourself. Watch cartoons, Oprah, movies. Do you notice bubbles of words overhead. Do you place all the blame for your awful circumstances on a terrible mother and father. Do you ever accuse poverty. Color. White people. Capitalism. The president. God. Terrorists. Yourself.

I am as guilty as the pretend movie we watch, Precious. Guilty of trying to put thoughts in your head. I can only guess what might be best for you to think or do. And my guesses probably wrong, corny, even if well-intentioned. Though one of my guesses is that everybody—like me, like you, Precious—must guess if they hope to sort through the enigma of being alive, adrift in a Yellow Sea.

An overload of information from buds stuffed in your ears. Hip-hop. Rap. Ads. Words from mothers, fathers, teachers, movies, books, politicians, preachers, TV. Too much and never enough. Especially when what feels crucially important inside matters not one iota to a world outside going about its busy, busy business. A world oblivious as the Yellow Sea. Movie of a life keeps steamrolling across the screen and you or I or the taxi driver can't stop it. Movie never pauses to ask: Hey, Precious. Am I getting it right.

After the bubble/clouds, clashes in the streets, the dying and crying, after blood spilled that fails to return Precious to us, after smoke clears and the neighborhood scraped clean, hosed down, we must take to the streets again. Eight of us exit a church. Preacher and mourners file out behind us. Eight of us, women and men, carrying a coffin. More pallbearers than usual and we would be more, but for the fact only so many fit alongside the coffin. Eight also because everyone's love and grief for Precious overflowing and the more of us who able to plant a shoulder under her oversize coffin, wrap a fist in one of its solid brass handles, the fewer left to walk alone, stand alone, empty-handed, hearts full, minds full of an unbearable burden and not a thing to do about it. Not even share the sad job of pallbearing Precious on her last trip through neighborhood streets. No comfort. Nothing for people in the sea of faces to do except bow their heads a moment, weep or pray or turn to stone when the coffin passes. Helpless witnesses one more time, squeezed into another vast throng packing a square, lining streets, avenues, alleys through which the funeral supposed to wind, how long, how long, past every crowded station. Past each individual mourner. Past each cluster and knot of folks who gather with the faint hope the coffin may pass with dignity the spot they occupy before the authorities descend or insupportable love, grief, and anger set people off to rampage the quarter.

Eight dressed in black—black gloves, shiny black shoes—eight because zigzag progress through the neighborhood will cover miles, consume hours, a lifetime maybe, so a good idea on a scorching day to include extra pairs of shoulders, hands, feet, and then if one of us totally exhausted, she or he can slack off a half minute and not exactly be missed, not set the litter lurching.

Not one dip or sigh or falter acceptable today in the cadence of our march. Our slow-motion surge through the streets. Easy, easy. Take her easy, people. Eight also because Precious quite large. A big big girl. Not just heavyset—heavy. Big and heavy. A load, you might as well go on and say if you got to go there. A load for four, eight, sixteen, a hundred pallbearers, even if it's only the memory of Precious inside the xxl, brass-fixtured, silk-lined, ebony coffin.

Not that I'm complaining. Just sharing plain truth from the point of view of one of eight brothers and sisters toting Precious. Child's heavy. Dust and ashes of Precious a load. Her absence a load. Precious gone, never be back. Weight not gone. We must bear the weight of her death, weight of our lives.

Knees about to buckle first step I took and I would have wiped out next step if I didn't remember the bubbles, the clouds. Remember to slide, glide as clouds instructed. Slide and glide the only way to get that solid lead coffin through the streets, up and down hills, across bridges, around corners, squeezed through skinny alleys, following an intricate map of the neighborhood we chant inside our heads. Not stepping or striding but a sort of slide/glide, feet barely touching the pavement, you know, like dancing salsa the proper way a Dominican guy had tried to teach me once, but I didn't catch on. Too much freelance and jitterbug in me back then.

Once we have her kind of hoisted up in the air, it becomes partly a matter of holding on tight, hoping Precious doesn't float away, and partly getting ready for the unbearable weight when she starts coming back down. We slip ourselves under her. Slip rope-a-dope out of her way. Fly her again when she's ready to fly.

Almost lose her every time. Lose her like the taxi driver loses his wife when he sends her alone across the Yellow Sea. Precious never stops shivering inside the coffin. Rolls from one side to the other as if she's small as a doll, but enough Precious weight in the empty box to drive with a single blow the spike of a tall, sturdy grown man like me down into the pavement till not even the crown of my head shaved bald in mourning shows.

Not about brute strength. It's about balance and sharing. We learn to count silently to ourselves and don't lose track. Tune our bodies to rock back and forth as Precious rocks back and forth. Learn her rhythm. Let it become ours so we always got her and she's got us.

A matter of silence and listening, as the clouds foretold. Of weave, of steady give and take of shoulders and hips and feet. Partly a group vibe, part solo. Alone. Not alone. Partly forgetting, partly remembering. Like almost dead one moment, alive the next. What it takes to keep from drowning in the Yellow Sea, from going down under killing weight.

> *THE IRREDUCIBLE MIRACLE IS . . . WE HAVE SUSTAINED EACH OTHER*

Going where. Going. Going. Old city gone. Harlem, Brooklyn, the Bronx, Queens, Wall Street, Battery Park, towers of steel and glass gone.

Each time I read a cloud, words hover like music above my head. Like music that plays at the end of *Precious*:

> *Took a long time to find this place . . . a long long time to recognize your face.*

BUNNY AND GLIDE

We are innocent. Our faces blacked up to make mischief not wreak havoc. Not hurt anybody. We are friendly masks. Your neighbors. Don't you almost hear our familiar names in the aliases we have assumed.

Innocent. Our wannabe dark color a final guarantee we are safe and you have nothing to fear. You can look right through our color if you choose and see our bright eyes, bright smiles, bright faces lighting up the darkness, yearning to play with you. Ghost dance with you. Not rob your piggy banks.

SNOW

He awakens. Goes to the window, opens the curtain, pulls up the shade, and sees snow. Remembers what it is. Where it is. Looks. No snow out the window last time he looked. Where has he been.

Asleep. Snowing as he slept. Not him snowing. It. Snow falling as he sleeps then awakens, outs himself from bed, pushes aside a curtain, pulls/draws up a shade/blind, and sees snow through the window. Sees through snow. Through himself making up a snow story. Sees snow begin after he pulled/drew down the blind/shade then closed the curtain across the window to make darkness for sleep. Sleep after his eyes close. Snow beginning before he awakens. While he slept in the dark. Falling. Snow falling. Darkness falling.

Snow older than his story. Older than him. He cannot go where it begins. He does not know where/when/how it begins or what it is he sees as he falls, falling, fallen, fell. Night's blackness. Snow's whiteness. There like the push of his bowels demands attention every morning. Snow one story he tells himself looking outside through the window. Through words. Through snow.

Sees through words as he sees through a window. As if words not there. As if they are not in the way. Like a window is there and not there if he sees through it when he awakens, pulls open the curtain, draws up, pulls up whatever else covers a window, to look out. Out there. There where he cannot know or go. What he looks at through a window, sees through words.

GHOST DANCER

Small, scraggly, begging bird ghost dances in margins of the little enclosed green space I call my garden until it gets my attention and I go inside to fetch crusts of bread I save to feed it. A kind of robin, I learn from Internet pictures. Not the fat, red-breasted American robin. Tiny robin the French call an orange-throated thrush.

It hops, darts, freezes. Sudden fits of hunger, fear, curiosity, greed. Hop-hopping, hip-hop it comes and goes or stops to profile, body slightly tilted towards me, a single black eye fixed on me. Dot ending a sentence. Then its head twitches, once, twice, side to side too fast to follow so the single eye directed at me, divided from the other by skull and beak, can show whatever's visible to its second eye.

Sustained fits of boldness often bring it close, hop-hopping along a trail of crumbs I sprinkle so it ends only inches from a lounge chair in which I settle myself. Close enough so I could stretch out my arm and reach down and pet the bird. Even closer if it chooses to hop up next to my hand on the chair's arm. That close, though I couldn't touch it, even if I tried. Too wary. Too fast. Eyes on mine. Quick pecks. Quick choices. Quick eye. Pick, peck-peck until it suddenly swoops away.

* * *

On a deserted stretch of beach near Toulindac I often sunbathe naked, and improbably, one day there's the bird. Far from my garden, atop a tall boulder whose color matches the bird's drab, mottled wing feathers. No doubt about it, same creature. Same meager size. Faded orange bib. Its beggar's beady eye. Hunger, fear, curiosity, greed. Same silent, spying questions it overhears me ask and I overhear it ask.

Mind elsewhere, my eyes see a bird on a rock. I'd been halfway dozing, sprawled on a towel on warm sand, thinking about nothing in particular besides clear blue sky, glittering sea I expected to greet my eyes each time I opened them to look around and luxuriate in the good luck that had brought me to that place, at that hour, that day. Reminding myself before I shut my eyes again to remember to write in my journal how the texture of certain mowed fields passed on the drive to Toulindac resembled the coats of vast, sleeping animals. Though many birds of various kinds frequent the beach, I wasn't watching them nor listening to their cries, no thoughts of birds or much of anything else in my mind when the small robin appears.

As usual it perches long enough—four, five seconds—to let me know it's there and sees me and knows I see it, belly empty or not, demanding to be filled. Same bird in a cove miles from my backyard, way, way too far away for it to range, and I understand, before it flies off, that back in my garden a hawk or cat or winter had gotten it.

COLLAGE

In this collage I want Romare Bearden to save the life of Jean-Michel Basquiat. It never happened. Or happened and no witness of the conversation between Bearden and Basquiat while they spray-paint graffiti in a vast graveyard of subway cars:

Do you believe writing changes a wall.

You mean make a wall fall down. Make a new wall. That what you mean.

Yeah. Different after we scratch on it. Different wall.

Gotta be.

How you know that. Who told you that.

We're different each time we write. You. Me. Wall gotta be.

Scratch on a wall, it belongs to us, right.

No. Huh-uh. Write on it, nobody owns it. Anybody walk right through it.

No wall, where's the writing.

Still there. Inside the other side.

You full of shit now. Talking shit now. Say any damned thing.

You're the one asking questions.

Not asking questions. Just want to know, is all.

Just write.

Sometimes I think you think you some kind of wall.

Keep scratching. Maybe you make me go away.

Sometimes I think you think you write on me.

Maybe scratch on your scratching, maybe. Not on you. Why you think I wanna make my main man go away.

I ain't nobody's damn wall.

That's what I'm talking about, main man.

You bout done, man.

Ready to split if you ready, main man.

Let's get the fuck gone. Scratching make me hungry.

One last lick. *Phziff.* Can empty. Done. Finished. And there. See it. A hungry mouth like yours. We outta here, main.

Main can sound like *man. Man* can sound like *main.* Trains overhead can sound like trains underground, Basquiat says to himself. Though trains can't fly. Though they sound like they up there in the sky. Like thunder. Can't see thunder either. Can't see trains underground either. They shake, rattle, roll. Invisible though you know they underfoot shake, rattle, rolling you and you think you see them, dark and invisible as it is under there. Like you see rumbles inside the stomach when you hungry. Like you know it's trouble coming. No money. No home. No food. How you spozed to eat if you don't go on and do wrong. How you spozed to write.

August Wilson, who grew up in Pittsburgh, Pennsylvania, wrote:

> *In Bearden I found my artistic mentor and sought, and still try to make my plays the equal of his canvases . . . I never had the privilege of meeting Romare Bearden. Once outside 357 Canal Street in silent homage, daring myself to knock on his door . . . sorry I*

didn't . . . often thought of what I would have said to him that day if I had knocked on his door and he had answered. I probably would have just looked at him. I would have looked and if I were wearing a hat, I would have taken it off in tribute.

Romare Bearden born September 2, 1911, in Charlotte, North Carolina. Jean-Michel Basquiat born December 22, 1960, in Brooklyn. Both men died in New York City on the twelfth day of different months in 1988. Bearden in March. Basquiat the following August. Basquiat resided at 57 Great Jones Street until a drug overdose killed him. Bearden's last address, 357 Canal Street, a short walk on the Lower East Side from Great Jones.

Romare Bearden, world-famous collagist, attended Peabody High, same public school in Pittsburgh my sister, my two dead brothers, my brother in prison for life, and I attended. Very same Bearden who heard from a friend that some artists at the beginning of the Italian Renaissance resisted demands of their patrons for paintings that conformed to fashionable rules of perspective mandated by the new science and math of rendering perspective. Artists feared deep cuts opening like doors into a canvas. Tintoretto, for example, screwed up on purpose. Believed illusory holes in a painting might become real holes into which the gaze, maybe the gazer's body and soul, might plunge and be lost forever. Who knows, Bearden says to Basquiat. Point is resist. Painters might tumble in, too.

Bearden's collages remind Basquiat of how his mother used to talk. Still talks on her good days. Her stories flatten perspective. Cram in everything, everyone, from everywhere she's been.

Spanish, her native language, and her English flow seamlessly, intimately when she's telling tales. Like the mix of materials Bearden combines to construct collage. Her words may be foreign, her accent unfamiliar, but listeners able to follow. Anecdotes she relates fill space to the brim without exhausting it. Moments she has experienced become large enough, thank goodness, to include everybody. Nobody feels left out.

Bearden's collage and Mom's narratives truly democratic—each detail counts equally, every part matters as much as any grand design. Size and placement don't highlight forever some items at the expense of others. Meaning depends upon point of view. Stop, Basquiat tells himself. I sound like a museum audiocassette guide when all I really want to say is *dance*. Mom talking story or Bearden at the turntable mixing cutouts with paint with fabrics with photos with empty spaces invite people to dance.

Basquiat loved to make music. Played in bands with his homies from scratching, hanging out. Jammed in clubs, recorded hours of tapes, their sound a mix of all the kinds of music they heard around them and noises in the streets, drug noises inside their heads. Basquiat disappointed when the band cooking and everybody in the audience too stoned to dance.

No one's fault, Romare Bearden supposes, if a gift he fashions doesn't quite fit in the box it was meant to fill with love. He tilts the collage board. Lets fragments he'd chosen slide back down to the worktable. Discovers they no longer fit there either. Collage board empty. Table overflowing. He must start again. Decide again what to include or discard. He believes his life depends on each choice. His feet shuffle beneath the worktable like Monk's feet under a piano. Working collage is too hard, impossible really, unless he hears something resembling music whose rhythms guide his eyes, hands.

Not surprising, given the scope of his ambitions, that Bearden misremembers occasionally the dimensions of a board he's preparing for collage or forgets how large a medley of ingredients he has assembled. Anyone observing him labor could have told him he's undertaking a doomed task. Too much on the table, limited room, after all, within a frame. Bearden's extremely smart so he knows better, too, but gets seduced by the privilege of paying absolute attention, piece by piece, to every item he selects. If pushed, he'd probably insist that losing track of the bigger picture a mercy, even a momentary state of grace, Bearden might add, especially when you are an older man. Why not linger over a swatch of antique Alabama patchwork quilt alive under his gaze as he rotates and rubs it, discovering new, mellow harmonies among its once brightly colored threads. Sweet funk of it, he brings it closer to his nose.

Collage should prepare brand-new space, Bearden says to Basquiat. I do not wish to abandon things I gather for collage into a space previous occupants own. I think collage envisions new pasts as well as new futures. Wonder if *thinking* is the proper word to express how I decide, separate, test.

Bearden recalls Alberto Giacometti lamenting a fatal skewering of attention as he sculpted the face of his brother Diego Giacometti. No matter how swiftly his eyes travel from flesh-and-blood brother to clay and back, Alberto wrote, he confronts the enigma of a Diego whose face changes. Never the face seen an instant before. Often the face of a stranger. Mysteriously troublingly to Giacometti, as my brother's face can appear to me after six months, nine, a year between visits to the prison.

Space framed within collage at least as elusive as any human face. Each time Bearden studies an element he considers adding to a collage—a color, a photo, a triangle of denim—the total composition vanishes. To see it whole again, his eyes must relinquish their grip on the element. Same way I lose my brother when I exit prison walls. The way I must exit the world outside prison bars to visit my brother.

Well, Basquiat asks, how does an artist resolve this dilemma, Maestro. This perpetual losing battle, this shifting back and forth, this absence, gap, this oblivion between a reality the senses seize and a reality the imagination seizes.

You guess. You believe, Bearden would respond to Basquiat or anyone else curious and serious enough to ask. A kind of wishful thinking, he might admit to himself. Each step of building collage precarious. Unleashes energy. Revelation. Loss. Grasping something concrete in your hand, you leave this *inextricable place*, as a fellow artist, Samuel Beckett, called it, and revisit a remembered place. You understand the fragment you grasp is as fragile, fallible as memory. Understand no former place remains fixed, unchanged. But you guess, believe a reunion will occur. Not in a space waiting patiently as a prison cell. A generously welcoming place, you hope.

* * *

Bearden worries about things that may have slipped off the worktable to the floor. He's unable to explain to Basquiat why removal of objects from an array sometimes makes the array more plentiful, not smaller. Nor can he explain how a board upon which he's arranging things becomes more spacious as he packs it. He learns to live with the necessity of letting go. Enjoys the idea of himself being as surprised as the stranger who opens one of these gift boxes he prepares.

Our eyes observe waves rippling the sea. But where exactly is a wave, Bearden winks and asks Basquiat. We can't see water molecules bobbing up and down. We think we see waves rippling. If my collages work, the stuff composing them gets agitated, makes waves.

Or you might say each collage starts with the bare bones of a story. For instance, me and two other colored boys beat up on Eugene, a crippled white boy. My grandmother intervenes, rescues the boy, and he becomes my best friend. Grandma discovers he lives in a brothel with his prostitute mother and rescues him again. He comes with his birds to stay in our house a short year then dies. A collage I built is layer upon layer of questions about that simple story.

Takes lots and lots of Angels and Devils hopping around to make a world anybody can see, Basquiat agrees. But where you spozed to put stuff that doesn't belong in the picture, he would ask Bearden. How you get a genie back in the bottle once the genie's out. What disease crippled poor Eugene. What names he give his birds. How much did Eugene's mom charge for a piece of pussy. What's her name. Did she earn more or less in a lifetime of selling herself than the price one of your collages or my paintings commands today. Rumor in the street says nobody survives. Who tries. Who asks.

There are about thirty words around you all the time, like *thread* and *exit*, Basquiat claimed.

I met a man who looked after Bearden in Bearden's old age when he was cancer-ridden, too weak to drive himself to his studio on Long Island City or climb stairs to the second floor of his apartment or handle heavy collage boards. Man told me Romare Bearden loved collards. Loved even more the pot liquor in which collard greens cooked. *Collards*, if you say it like the man said it, sounds like *coloreds* and *coloreds* sounds like *collards.* Bearden a gentle, easy person to care-take, the man told me and being with the old, dying artist probably best time of the man's life, he confides, smiling as he recalled their long conversations he taped, how scared he was carrying Bearden piggyback up and down steps. But you best not forget that bowl of pot liquor to start Romare's day. Evil all day when no cup of steaming collard juice first thing.

More than once found myself up at 4:00, 5:00 A.M., the man said, cooking collards so the liquor could simmer down a couple hours to where it would taste just right by the time Mr. and Mrs. B up and I had him washed, shaved, dressed, and ready at his little table kind of desk in the workroom downstairs. Most days I made sure some leftover liquor in the pot to save and heat up next morning, but to tell the God's truth, I was getting old, too. Worried I'd stumble with him on my back and kill us both on those damned steps. Getting older every day along with Mr. Bearden. Starting to forget things with so much to do to keep his days running smooth and regular the way he liked it. Every day he could manage the trip, I'd drive him out to Long Island City. Be in the studio by noon working with Teabo, his assistant.

Sometimes I'd wake up in my bed, *Oh, shit*, and remember the greens pot empty on the stove. *Damn.* Too poor to ever own a watch when I was growing up. Taught myself to keep time in my head. Could tell you the minute and hour, just as good as if a watch on my wrist. Must have been born with the gift of a clock in my head or maybe I figured out I'd have one if I made a habit of paying attention. Won a whole lot of bets in college with that trick. Could tell you the time today. And still wake up at exactly the time I tell myself before I go to sleep. Wide awake, no alarm, no watch. Part of the gift, I guess. Me and time always been on good speaking terms, you might say, so when I remembered an empty pot on his stove, I'd know the hour and, *Oh, shit, man.* Get your big behind out the bed, man. Go fix Romare's greens so they be simmered down perfect—greasy, salty, tiny bits of grit in the juice, too strong for most people, but just how he liked it.

Basquiat owned an illustrated encyclopedia of signs and symbols that included signs hobos chalked and scratched on small town walls to warn other hobos. Basquiat often drew on his paintings the hobo sign meaning "nothing to be gained here" or the sign meaning "a beating awaits you here."

* * *

Once upon a time, Basquiat says to Bearden, I painted the Devil on a door to scare myself away. *Go Away, fool.* Never come back here again and stand here staring at this damned drug-den door. And fuck sure never again knock. And if you hear steel bolts unbolted, don't you dare push it open and walk through to where you know the Devil's crouched down inside, nasty, hairy, bare black ass all up in your face first thing you see in there. Devil bent down munching on garbage inside dead people's stomachs.

Basquiat thinks he scratched not painted the goddamn door. Samo again. Scratching again. Never will be a painter. Always Samo. *Samo* sounds like *Sam O.* Means S-O-S: Same Ole Shit. Same ole Samo. Never not Samo. Means help me. Means help Samo. Samo. Samo. Stuck like a record. Samo over and over. Or Samo maybe sounds like *Sa Mo*, and means some more. Like Devil, please give Samo some more. *Gimme s' mo.* Samo wants s' mo.

Samo scratching Devil on a door. Ugly door. Ugly Devil. Paints words in the Devil's ugly mouth. Words in his red, empty eye-hole tunnels. Go away, fool. Go away, Samo. Go away, Devil. Go away. No more. Never again, Samo. For Samo's sake do not enter. Do not forsake. Don't just go away, Samo. Run, nigger, run. Far away. Way. Way. But rumor in the street says you are Samo. Always. Scratcher not painter. You cannot change. Why in hell would you want to change anyway, even if the fool you are could change. *Samo* sounds like *S' mo.* Gotta git me some more.

Confess. You the same Samo. Confess to the few who would listen. As if any fool would listen to Samo. Samo who can't paint.

Samo scratching. *Scratch* one of Devil's names. *Scratch* means graffiti. *Scratch* means money. Means itch. Means fuck wit a record. Kill it. Same ole itch. Scratch it. Scratch buys a bag. Ten bags a day. Hundred. Here's s' mo, Samo. More scratch than you can count. Devil on the door. Behind the door. Sees you. Loves to see you coming. Everybody loves you, Samo. You the man.

Wuzzup, Dude. Wuzzup, Money. Wuzzup, Main Man. They can see you through the door. See through you. Watch you ache to paint the door shut. Shut. Shut. Shoot. Shooted. Shut away. Shoot away. Paint away the Devil. No. Not paint. Scratch. Roll of bills in your fist like a chunk of bloody bandages.

Devil means money means bags and bags of dope. As many bags as dead bodies stashed inside the door. They watch you. Dead eyes looking through the wooden door at you. Staring. Waiting. Scratching. They love you. Funny, you think. Run, you think. You want to paint it shut forever. Paint Devil on it, inside it forever.

Devil on door grins back at you. Thinks it's funny, too, Samo. Same ole Samo. Funny Samo. Funny Devil. Dead eyes see you push through. Not a door. It's a window, a mirror. Glass breaking. You fall through. Glass everywhere. Nails falling down like rain. Knives. You are falling. Down you go flat on your black skinny ass. Funny. You crack up. No. You step through. Glass slippery under bare toes. Step on a crack break your mama's back. You hip-hop, whistle, snap your fingers, wiggle, squirm through untouched. To the other side. Samo.

Giddy-up, Jean-Michel Basquiat hollers. Rides a good horse he owns. Own all this, too, he thinks. This Paradise on this island where he bounces in the saddle, astride a thoroughbred Arabian, nigger-colored horse. Giddy-up. Giddy-up, cowboy. As far as the eye can see owns waves of green of sea of clouds of blue sky above and below him owns the hooves of the animal squeezed between his knees, his thighs be-dumping, be-dumpety-dumping in a place called Hawaii he believes where sits this island he owns, rides and nobody can see him, bother him. He owns it, all of it, all of this place stretching to a horizon that shimmers, bobs out there, as far as he's able to see. Finish line floats out there somewhere, finished like a painting stretched wet to dry on its frame of spears, a horizon opening as a dream stretches open. You clomp, clomp closer and closer to it, through it, and beyond each time you reach it forever.

There are about thirty words around you all the time . . . all of them DEVIL.

Perhaps it's 1986 when Basquiat watches a fine young French thing pedal past, bare-legged on her bicycle. She's K, a lady I will meet fifteen years or so later, marry eventually, long after that momentary encounter between notorious Jean-Michel Basquiat's eyes and hers.

His eyes on her nice, tanned legs, big, cute frizzy hair, sweet hips, and lips that speak French, mother tongue of Jean-Michel's father. A sure-enough fox, petite like he prefers, graced by that perfection nature reserves for smallish, compact women's bodies like hers. She's wearing short shorts that day. Then he sees her everywhere on the Lower East Side—Mudd Club, Studio 54, Area—and she sees him and sees he's very aware of seeing her she's sure. They are very aware of each other she's sure, and he sure is, too. They speak briefly sometimes in passing. Greetings, smiles exchanged usually always except when he's doing sullen or lost in space or mounted on his gray Dürer death horse or plain sleepy from no sleep for days or plain high or testing maybe if it's true he's truly, truly famous, beyond fame, everybody who's somebody or not recognizes him and counts coup whether or not he notices them or nods or looks back or not or mocks like a blackface minstrel with a wiggly tongue their stares.

He notices her and she notices cute, brown him everywhere around LES until one night in Area when he waves her over she goes as far as to stand smiling beside the table where he sits with an older man, and though the painter doesn't know her name he halfway introduces, halfway pimps her in a teasing, funny way she thinks to the dapper man who turns out to be his Haitian father.

Quick, hot surge of jealousy, envy of the Devil flashing in Basquiat's eye as I listen, but just as instantly I'm pleased, profoundly grateful beyond words for brightness in K's eyes while she reminisces about her encounters with a famous artist. My wife who has been suffering brutal insomnia, her gaze, her affect dulled by the wages of sleeplessness, despair, and anxiety over a string of deaths, of sudden serious illnesses striking family and closest friends, her own increasingly frequent attacks of tachycardia and other ominous, unresolvable threats to her health, so of course I worry with her, about her. No, not worry. I quake inside with fear I may be losing her. Thus losing everything. Though I must believe, must trust, trust, trust her mind's deep-down toughness, her small body strong as a horse.

On the worst days I launch endless searches for reassuring signs of our former, familiar selves. Walk for hours alone to empty my head of anything except the effort, the noise of my footsteps through this dreary time capsule of a latter-day Lower East Side, this remnant of a boundless universe we once roamed together. Boy wonder, colored painter, victim, heir, wife, husband, kids, scratchers, thieves, flirtatious Haitian fathers, all of us, the fallen and survivors, coloreds and not, then and now, too many to count or keep track of, or touch or talk with. Bridges and high-rises, ghettos, music, fashion, meatpacking districts, financial districts, hi-line, traffic, parks, news, ethnic and religiously cleansed slums, and racialized enclaves battered, bruised, cowering. Foreign nations collapsing here, bleeding, museums, sprawl of new construction, prisons, galleries, cell phones, war, murder, terrorists.

Who dat. Who she. Pedaling down Spring Street. Crazy little French mama come *Knock/Knockin* at my front door. *Bon jour. Bonjour.* Not the Devil, are you, you French sweetie pie. Open up and let me in, Samo almost scratches on the door, the window, the mirror within which he sees her welcoming eyes, sees his. Sees the grinning Devil's face.

The door a forgery, experts almost unanimously agree. Wannabe. Imposter. Fraud. If the original Jean-Michel Basquiat ever painted a Devil on the door of a dope den or even just scratched one, this ain't it. Clearly the work of another, obviously inferior artist, opines one expert, and not only am I certain, he adds for spite and to needle his colleagues, I happen to know the person's name whose work it is. Guy even admitted it to me, risked forfeiting the million or so door was worth if he claimed it as his. Says he's an admirer of the great Basquiat. Knew him back in the day, on the street, the scratching scene. Frequented same dealers, dope joints, etc. Sorry Samo dead, he said. Miss him. Bad luck to diss him, said my informant. But he winked, and added that the rumor on the street is boy never painted anything anyway. Samo a scratcher. Keeps on scratching. Once a scratcher, always a scratcher. Ask Samo. If you can stand the look on his face. Looks like the Devil when he grins. Bad grill. Gaps. Bad speckled, bumpy, pimply skin. Bad color. Bad boy smile when he looks at you says, Hi. I'm spooky Samo. No way you'd believe he had it all once, looking at him today. Half dead. Or dead. Depending on which expert you believe.

Ask the Authentication Committee organized, authenticated by his colored West Indian daddy. They/he determine who, when, what comes and goes through gallery doors and how much it goes for. And what goes *phizzz* in the night because nobody loves it. Committee makes paintings real. Not scratch. Not not worth squat. They decide what's art. They make Samo real. Same ole Samo. Stamped with Samo Copyright Stamp.

To this collage of conversations, which perhaps never took place, let me add one more. Behind bars of a ten-by-ten-inch, four-inch-deep stainless steel rack anchored low on our bathroom wall—packed, squeezed so tightly not one more could fit—K, my wife of twelve years, saves, for reasons known only to her, old copies of French home decorating magazines. On two covers—*Elle Décoration* (nov-2014) and *Marie Claire Maison* (fev-mars-2012)—are phrases that struck and stayed with me as I browsed through K's collection while I sat on the toilet. In my mind many times since, I've cut out and pasted up the phrases. Formed them into an exchange that very likely could have occurred between two extremely smart, curious, intense young people. Two immigrants, wayfaring strangers in the teeming metropolis of NYC circa 1986:

N'ayez Plus Peur de Noir
Petits Espaces/Grande Idées

In the spirit of English editions of Tolstoy's novel *War and Peace* that supply translations of the French Tolstoy liberally mixes with his Russian, I offer translations of the French words above that captured my attention:

Fear Black No More
Great Ideas for Small Spaces

Since I'm unsure who thought which thought, I won't attach speakers' names to the phrases. Anyway, in their original arrangement of bright colors and a variety of fonts on glossy magazine covers that first caught my eye, the French words express ideas no one in particular owns. Thus I float or rather scratch those words here, a collage in this collage, above the heads of K and Basquiat, not as evidence the thoughts were ever spoken aloud by either of them, but as thoughts that belong to them—embedded, released in conversations their eyes struck up.

One luxury of growing old, Bearden says to Basquiat, says it a bit shyly, self-consciously, since he knows Basquiat will not get very old, is more time to ask questions about simple stories. Stories that make us up as we make them up. Will I be born again. Alive again once this particular allotment of years runs out. Is a city called Pittsburgh still reachable by catching a train north from Mecklenburg, North Carolina, or a train south from Harlem that passes through Philadelphia then climbs over and tunnels through many mountains, rounds a gigantic horseshoe curve. If Pittsburgh continues to exist—a golden triangle cordoned by bridges and three rivers, clinging to steep hills like Rome—and if I reach Pittsburgh and walk its streets, am I a boy there or old like I am here and now, still asking a boy's questions. Is teasing my nearly bald head with such idle speculations a less forgivable luxury now than when I was a kid. Am I stuck forever, man or boy, with a bad habit, perhaps, of wasting precious time daydreaming. As if living and questioning never ends, as if a simple question might stump time, buy time, stop time long enough for a boy, a man, to slip past the conductor and ride back and forth to Pittsburgh on a beam of light without paying the price of a ticket.

Anyway, Romare Bearden confides, my first drawings, like your Devil on a door, not very nice. I learned from my friend Eugene how to draw nasty stuff we spied through rotting floorboards of the attic he shared with his mother over a whorehouse that sat down Spring Street and around the corner from my grandmother's boardinghouse. One Saturday afternoon Grandma saw us extremely busy, busy, drawing on big, greasy, blood-speckled sheets of paper chickens came wrapped in from the butcher shop, and she marched over: What you boys up to. Why you so quiet over here. When she saw what we were up to, her eyes got wide.

She hollered. Snatched our drawings. Ripped them up and rained the tiny pieces into the kitchen garbage pail.

I expected a good whack or two. My grandmother one of those pillow-bosomed women who love children dearly, especially me, but when you made her mad, watch out. Pow. Trouble was Grandma so nice and easy most the time you don't notice her getting mad. First sign of mad. Pow. Then it's too late to move out her way cause with Grandma getting mad also a matter of getting even. Fact is I didn't exactly understand why she might be hitting mad when I saw her coming over to where we were busy at the kitchen table, though I sort of knew the pictures Eugene and I were drawing had something very secret, very private about them I surely didn't want Grandma of all people to see.

What I had peeked at between the raggedy floorboards had scared me, main man. People hurting one another my first thought. Noisy, ugly thrashing about. Mean grabbing, mean pushing and squeezing, spilled whiskey, dirty sheets, cigarettes. Bare skin of grown-up body parts I'd never seen so naked before. More scary because it was colored bodies and white bodies down there mixed up closer than I had ever seen colored and white mixing on Spring Street and in the little checkerboard patches of neighborhood around Spring around the rolling mill where a few lucky colored folks had regular jobs. All kinds of people living in the neighborhoods. Poor the only requirement. Mixing on one hand but on the other hand definitely not mixing. No trespassing the Golden Rule. Only colored men rented my grandmother's rooms, and different houses, different blocks, different barbers, different churches for white and colored because people believed in sticking to their own kind. Even kids believed it, so the first time I met up with Eugene, it was me, Mumps, and Bo, the three of us teasing then beating on him unmercifully because what the hell a white boy think he's doing standing there staring at us, him ugly as a fresh knot on somebody's head got conked by a rock. Probably him being crippled as much as being the wrong color (though my skin wore almost the same color, by the way) made us jump him, smack him down so he'd go away and never bring his pitiful self back to our alley behind Spring where Mumps, Bo, and me played.

My grandmother busted in that time, too. Set down her shopping bags on the cobblestones, yelled, Stoppit. Stop that, you bad boys, and whacked whoever she could lay her hands on, running us away from that skinny white kid. Whacking Mumps and Bo like she whacked me because that's how it worked back then around Spring Street. You were everybody your color's child and if you got caught doing wrong by any colored adult friendly with your people, they had the right to whip your behind and send you home for another good beating because you should know better and not shame yourself, not shame your family by doing wrong in public as if you hadn't been raised to know better.

Anyway, going back to the other, later time after she tore up those butcher paper drawings and shredded them or maybe burned them to ashes in the kitchen sink, Grandma calmed down and asked me and Eugene what in Jesus name did we think we were doing and where did we get the idea of those terrible pictures. We told her about the room under the attic room Eugene lived in with his mother, about a spy hole in one corner of the floor covered over by just a ratty piece of linoleum we lifted to check out the action below. Told Grandma in which particular house Eugene resided around the corner from Grandma's, the house I went to almost every day after school and many evenings, too, if Grandma said okay.

My, oh, my. Good Lord have mercy, Grandma groaned and snatched Eugene by the hand after she let go the ear she was pinching, and he gimped off beside her, though I know Eugene didn't hardly want to go home but he knew he better go with her and did, dragging his bad leg to slow things down as much as he dared without letting on he was scared or stubborn or just plain didn't want to go. But off he went with Grandma and when she came back to our house, I was surprised to see she still had Eugene by the hand and he got a little plaid, cardboard suitcase and Grandma carrying his birdcages and Eugene stayed with us till he got sick and passed.

Nineteen twenty-seven the year Eugene buried, Bearden says, and in 1978 I tried to pack all that Eugene story and Homewood, East Liberty, Pittsburgh story, the whole damned known world and probably the unknown, too, Bearden smiles, into a 16¼-inch by 20½-inch collage pasted on board I titled *Farewell Eugene.* All those worlds as they appeared to me fifty years afterwards in my memories of how crowded a time, a city, a boy's universe can be at any moment once you teach yourself to look closely and practice patiently for a lifetime the skills of cutting and pasting, gluing down textures, colors, fabrics, layer after layer to picture what the past may have been and how it rises again, solid and present as the bright orange disc of sun I put at the top-right corner of *Farewell Eugene.*

Same sun shining almost red over Eugene's funeral fifty years before with everybody on earth in attendance or at least nobody missing who should be there. Eugene's friends, his people, mine, his pigeons, Grandma, me, we're all there in the crowd back then and this time, too, if I got the collage close to right. All of us remembered, revived beneath an orange sun coloring the city, coloring flowers Eugene's pale mother holds that day. Same old sun, same old Pittsburgh, same old simple questions asking to be asked. The crowd of us then and now, living and dead saying our goodbyes, our hellos to Eugene. As many of us you might say as boarded Noah's Ark or as many as in the number religious thinkers in the Middle Ages used to bicker over if asked how many angels fit on the head of a pin.

Expectations

Some view our sable race with scornful eye,
"Their colour is a diabolical die."
Remember, *Christians, Negros,* black as *Cain,*
May be refin'd, and join th' angelic train.

—PHILLIS WHEATLEY, FROM "ON BEING BROUGHT FROM AFRICA TO AMERICA," IN *POEMS ON VARIOUS SUBJECTS, RELIGIOUS AND MORAL* (LONDON, 1773)

I expect shorter days. I expect war. I expect winter, felt winter's ghost present in July heat when scudding clouds hid the sun and a fall chill rode the air momentarily yesterday as I walked where I walk many days, a path marked by two parallel scars of bare earth about seven, eight feet apart which frame a slightly mounded seam of open ground—fleeced bright green by grass in spring—obviously a trail left behind by tire tracks on an unpaved back road frequently used once, abandoned now, except to serve as a double-rutted footpath of gravelly stones and hard-packed dirt thru farmer's fields, through pastures, through patches of forest common in Brittany, stands of very old, tall trees along the coast or here, inland, separating one small town or village from the next, leftover woods, leftover road edged by wire fencing or a single strand of wire, barbed, electrified perhaps, stretched between wooden posts, or the path lined by a dense wall of foliage, head high, scraggly hedges, bushes, or passes under branches and leaves that form a canopy, darkness beneath it, and sometimes if I'm looking far ahead in the direction I'm going, the two bare tracks and lane of cleared space between them disappear where the road bends sharply or dips after it climbs a rise of rolling countryside, or the old road, surrounded by forest, seems to enter a tunnel that continues endlessly beyond its circular mouth of shadow and floating spots of light, path obscured or consumed or both by unstill brightness and darkness, a path no longer on the ground, but hovering in air, and as I follow it, I do not expect to see anyone I know, only the rare walker or jogger coincidental as I am, a mirage like seasons that come and go each step I take.

I expect color to be used against me. I repudiate color, refuse color, and if I call any color mine, I am mistaken because it belongs to others, to people who use color against me, a color not my color, but something they call color, call me, a name for me, or rather many, many names for me, as many as there are many colors or many shades of a single color, as if the color they call me by is one that separates colored me clearly, finally, beyond doubt or correction from them, from the color they call themselves, from all other colors that my color is not, nor was, nor ever will be. I expect the difference of a color others say is mine, color they claim to see coloring me, will forever serve only purposes they perceive as beneficial to them, even though they may understand quite clearly that achieving those purposes harms me. I expect difference to be preserved by color the way any idea or limit or border or rule can be determined and settled by law, once and for all, absolutely, fatally, no exceptions, if law is empowered and imposed by irresistible force and force is empowered by law, the circles of force as law, of color as difference unbroken. Unbreakable bonds if I commit the error of calling myself a color or calling myself colored.

I expect that in order to continue to expect, continue to walk, think, and breathe, I must have water, air, food, shelter. I expect that without them I would expect nothing, I would be nothing, or be as close to being nothing as I am able to conceive or I wish to conceive or wish to bother myself attempting to conceive, since while I am something, whatever else I might be is inconceivable to me, except as nothing, except as not me, and what would that make of me, if I am nothing, if I am unable to expect, unable to find myself anywhere, except nowhere, nothing, what would be the point of trying to go there, to be nothing there, nothing in an imaginary world truly unimaginable, if no air, water, food, shelter, no expectations.

I expect to miss my right hand if I lose it. Expect my left hand, if I lose my right hand, not to miss it. The parts of my body strangers to one another. A body constituted of millions and millions of minuscule parts, each part selfish, oblivious. Dedicated, obliged to perform a single option, a simple act of on/off, yes/no, an act that perpetuates saying yes or no/on or off and nothing more. No idea of connection, dependence, no notion of an entity other than itself, nor of itself, no awareness, of course, of a particular body to which it belongs, a mortal body within which it functions, a body determining the life and death of each of the body's parts, every microscopic part or combination of parts such as a right hand or left hand I have learned to call mine and would miss terribly—perhaps more terribly even than if I lost someone I believed was the love of my life—if I lost either one of my hands, but a hand means nothing to other body parts, just as the parts mean nothing to themselves, no consciousness, each governed only by the simplest set of rules—on or off/yes or no—concerned by only a single function eternally or instantaneously, once or infinite repetitions, no difference for them. Still I willingly host this horde of strangers, autonomous and greedy and treacherous and temporary as each part is, I welcome them, embrace them call them my body. And nothing is closer, more intimate to me than my own body. We are identical. Without it I would be no one, nothing, and not to care about my body, not to love it first, last, always, or to neglect it, forget it, not only unwise, not only the beginning of madness and dissolution, but next to impossible because I am the signals sent to me by senses that constitute my flesh and blood, that animate my thoughts, the continuing presence constituting me.

Odd. I expect my body to follow me or me to follow it. Inseparable. One perhaps. Necessity perhaps. United against a world that is as unaware, as unconcerned about me as each part is of every other part.

I expect the blindness of one part to another part won't end. I expect the lie of color not to cure blindness.

I expect Nat Turner. I expect he will die again for the sin of color.

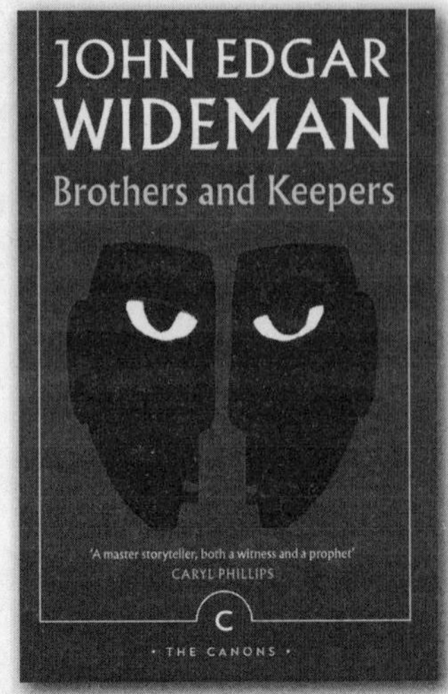

'Wideman's writing is so pure and convincing that he can break the rules of classical storytelling, even invent some new ones'

Boston Globe

CANONGATE